THE CLOCKMAKER'S SECRET

THE SLIM HARDY MYSTERIES #2

JACK BENTON

For Brandon Hale

an inspiration

THE CLOCKMAKER'S SECRET

1

THE HIKE WASN'T GOING TO PLAN.

The looming granite stacks of Rough Tor were a poor compass marker, shifting along the skyline as Slim Hardy attempted to realign himself with the trace of path which had led him up the hill from the car park.

To his right a small herd of wild moorland ponies blocked the direct route to the ridgeline and the tallest stacks. Their defiant eyes watched every step as Slim skirted around, moving slowly over the boggy, uneven terrain, wary of the granite scree poking through the tuffs of moorland grass.

Slim sighed. He was way off course now, Rough Tor's long ridge rising almost straight on, and the flat peak of Brown Willy with its sprinkling of rocks appearing straight ahead across a wide, gentle valley. He reached by habit for the hip flask that was no longer there, shook his hand as though to punish himself for his forgetfulness, then sat on a rock to take a breather.

Up on the ridge, the two hikers he had followed from the car park jumped down from among the rocks and headed on towards Brown Willy. As they disappeared from sight, Slim felt a sudden pang of loneliness. At the very bottom of the slope, there were three cars in the car park alongside the blur of red that was his pushbike, but of the other walkers there was no sign. Besides the ponies, he was alone.

After a bite of a leftover sandwich and a swig from a water bottle, Slim looked up at the peak, torn by indecision. He had a long cycle ride ahead of him down winding, potholed country lanes, and the battery in his light was flat. As he turned, though, the sun briefly broke through the clouds, and far to the south the English Channel glittered between two hills. To the northwest Slim looked for the Atlantic, but a bank of clouds hung low over the fields, obscuring all but the tiniest triangle of grey that might have been water.

With a persevering grunt he shouldered his rucksack and got back to the hike, but had taken no more than a few steps when a loose rock rolled under his boot, plunging him knee-deep into a pit of grimy water. Grimacing, Slim pulled his foot free of the bog and staggered forward onto drier ground.

As he removed and emptied his left boot, he gave a wistful grin, remembering that a spare pair of socks lay on the bed in his room, left out of his bag to make space for an old paperback from the guesthouse's borrowing shelf.

Again the sun briefly emerged from the clouds, the granite stacks sparkling in the sudden brightness. The herd of ponies had moved across the hill, leaving Slim with a straight route to the ridgeline.

'Come on,' he muttered to himself. 'Not a quitter, are you?'

His boot squelched as he pulled it back on, but with a grimace rarely leaving his face, he finally made it to the ridgeline fifteen minutes later, clambering up the granite stacks to the highest viewpoint. Fog had rolled in, obscuring everything but the slopes of the hill. The old China clay quarries to the southwest were ghosts in the fog, but beyond a murky grey sheet hung over the world.

With the water's grit like sandpaper between his toes, Slim paused only long enough to take a quick drink before beginning his downward journey. A warm early spring day was quickly reverting to a late winter evening, and only an hour of light remained before complete darkness. Even though the fog hadn't yet absorbed the little gravel car park into its amorphous grey palette—a speck of red near the lower wall identified his bike—it looked a lot further than the peak had seemed when he was starting out.

He was staring off into the distance, counting the sheep huddled into a natural bowl further down the slope as a way of putting the chill gusts of wind out of his mind, when something shifted under his foot.

He fell hard, catching himself with his hands. He had fallen on the same foot, but this time he turned his ankle, and a blistering pain raced up his leg. He rolled on to his back, eased off his boot and sat rubbing his ankle for a few minutes. Removing his sodden sock revealed the beginnings of an angry bruise, and the exposure to the air sent February chills through his body. The ground here was at least dry, and he sat up and stared upslope, feeling both angry and stupid. *Fool me once, fool me twice,* he remembered the beginning of a saying his ex-wife had been fond of, although he had forgotten the rest.

He looked around, wondering which rock had tripped him, and frowned. Something poked up between two tufts of grass, fluttering in the breeze.

The corner of a plastic bag, shredded and frayed, its old colour long faded to a grey-white. Slim hesitated before making to pick it up, remembering his tour of Iraqi with the Armed Forces, when such a thing might have indicated a landmine, a marker for local militants still using the area. Every bit of rubbish could have meant death, and in the suburbs of some dirty, dusty towns, Slim had barely dared take a forward step.

To his surprise, it resisted his sharp tug. He pushed his hands into the turf and eased his fingers around the hard, angular shape the bag contained. It spread out beneath the turf, a couple of hand spans across, and his heart began to race. Lost military ordinance? Dartmoor, to the northeast, was used for army drills, but Bodmin Moor was supposedly safe.

He pressed a finger into the hard surface, and it gave a little. Wood, not plastic or metal. No bomb he had ever known had been made from wood.

He pulled back turf that yielded easily and twisted the wrapped object out of the grass. Square corners and carved grooves aroused his curiosity. He untied the knot on the bag and withdrew the object inside.

'Huh…?'

The bag contained a beautiful, ornate cuckoo clock. Delicate wooden carvings surrounded a pretty central clock face. To his surprise it was still functioning, as a little cuckoo suddenly blasted out of a door above the 12-numeral, its cry a tired puff into Slim's stunned ears.

'WILL YOU BE STAYING ON ANOTHER WEEK, Mr. Hardy?

Mrs. Greyson, the stern-faced elderly landlady of Lakeview Bed & Breakfast, an establishment which lived up to only two of its three labels, was waiting in the gloomy hall when Slim entered through the front door. Cold and aching from the long ride, and still spooked from how close a swerving Escort with a blown-out engine had come to reducing him to mincemeat, he had hoped to avoid a confrontation until he had at least taken a shower.

'I haven't decided yet,' he said. 'Can I let you know tomorrow?'

'It's only that I need to know whether to advertise your room.'

Slim had seen no other customers in the four-room B&B. He forced a smile for Mrs. Greyson, but as he started past her for the stairs, he paused.

'Say, you don't know of anywhere locally that does valuations, do you?'

'Valuations? Of what?'

Slim lifted his wrist and waved the generic watch he had picked up in a Boots sale a year ago. 'Thought I might pawn this,' he said. 'I was thinking it might be time for an upgrade.'

Mrs Greyson wrinkled her nose. 'I can tell you how much that's worth. Nothing.'

Slim smiled. 'I'm serious. It belonged to my father. It's a family heirloom.'

Mrs Greyson shrugged as though aware he was spinning a lie. 'I'm sure you'd be wasting your time, but if you're really serious, you'll find somewhere in Tavistock. They have a market every Saturday. It sells all kinds of junk, and no doubt you'd find someone willing to take that off your hands for a very small fee.'

'Tavistock? Where's that?'

'Other side of Launceston. In Devon.' This last was said with a wrinkled nose, as though to exist beyond the Cornish border was the most heinous of crimes.

'Is there a bus?'

Mrs Greyson sighed. 'Why don't you just rent a car? What kind of person comes to Cornwall without a car?'

The kind who no longer has a driver's license, Slim wanted to say, but didn't. Her prejudices ran deep enough already without knowledge of his drink-driving ban.

'I told you, I'm trying to be environmentally sensitive. I'm attempting to get in touch with my earthly side.'

'How nice for you.' Another sigh. 'Well, there's a

timetable pinned to the door of your room, as I've told you before.'

Slim didn't remember whether she had told him or not. True, there was something, but it was faded to near illegibility and most likely years out of date.

'Thanks,' he said, giving her a smile.

'Honestly, you don't know how lucky you are now that First Bus has started operating in North Cornwall. Used to be, there was only one bus to Camelford all week. It left at two p.m. on Tuesday and you had to wait a week to get home again. Imagine getting stuck in Camelford for a week? An hour's enough for most people.'

'That bad, is it?'

Mrs. Greyson missed Slim's gentle sarcasm. 'They've been after a bypass for years. At least now the buses go twice a day. That was Blair, that was, sorted it out. Things have gone downhill since the Tories got back in. They were after the sea pool at Bude, then the public toilets in—'

'Thank you, Mrs. Greyson,' Slim said.

Mrs. Greyson turned back towards the kitchen, mouth still moving silently as though words continued to fall out like drips from a leaking tap, her hands clumsily shuffling a clutch of bills and bank statement envelopes. Slim had just begun to hope the conversation was over when she stopped and turned back. 'Will you be going out for dinner again tonight?'

Penleven had a single shop that shut at six p.m., and a single pub that stopped serving food at eight-thirty. He had half an hour to make it to his lonely table in the family room or it was a Cup Noodle and a tuna sandwich for the third night in a row. While Slim had his reasons for his extended stay in Cornwall, living up to his nickname wasn't one of them.

He nodded. 'I think I will,' he said.

'Well, don't forget your key,' she said, something she had said to him every night of his three-week stay. 'I'm not getting up to let you back in.'

3

Up in his neat, surprisingly large room for a house that was outwardly rather small, Slim took the bundled clock out of his rucksack and unwrapped it from the plastic bag.

He knew nothing about clocks. His last flat had contained a single cheap plastic one the previous occupant had left behind, and to tell the time he invariably used his old Nokia or a succession of bargain bin wristwatches until they were scratched beyond readability.

The clock was a wooden rectangle designed like a winter lodge, with a pointed, overhanging roof and a hole in the bottom for an absent pendulum. The clock face, with its metal roman numerals that were slightly tainted, was surrounded by swirls and carvings: animal and tree designs, symbols that perhaps represented the sun and moon or seasons. In a semi-circle beneath the clock face was a thin strip resembling a moon tilted upwards, or perhaps an unfinished horseshoe. A few illegible scratches had been made in its surface. The whole clock had been coated with a thick varnish primer coat, one to be sanded and smoothed away as the design was finalized and refined.

Slim gave a bemused shake of his head. He had never encountered a handmade clock before. If someone had taken the time to create something so complex, why wrap it up in a bag and bury it on the moor?

Interestingly, despite the lack of a pendulum it was still ticking, even though the hands were a couple of hours off correct time—it was now showing nearly eleven—and the bottom was badly water-damaged where the bag had ripped open. Slim tried to take the back off to look inside, but it was screwed tight, and with no tools of his own he didn't want to bother Mrs. Greyson again before morning. The wood, though, had the burned dirt smell of peat, as well as an aged mustiness. Slim could easily believe the clock was older than his own forty-six years.

Slim fetched a damp cloth from the corner washbasin and gave the clock a wipe down. The varnish quickly reached an imperious shine as grit and dust came away. Details in the carvings became more apparent: mice, foxes, badgers and other staples of British wildlife hiding among the filed curves and arcs of trees. With the firm click of the clock mechanism suggesting a mechanical knowhow equal to the artistic, whoever had built this clock had done it with great pride and an exceptional level of skill.

Slim set the clock up on the dresser beside his bed then fetched his coat. It was time for his nightly trek out to the local pub, hopefully in time to catch the last food orders. He didn't feel like a Chicken & Mushroom Pot Noodle for the third night in a row. It wasn't that he hated Pot Noodles, it was that the village's little shop only stocked the one flavour. On the one night he had leveled up and bought a tin of beans and sausages, he had found it to be three months out of date.

As he headed out into the light drizzle that was a mainstay of Bodmin Moor and its surrounds after nightfall, he couldn't stop thinking about the clock.

Had he found a bag of gold, it couldn't have been more mysterious.

4

'SO, WHO ARE YOU, REALLY, MR. HARDY?' MRS. Greyson said, holding back his breakfast plate as though its delivery were reliant on his answer. 'I mean, you stay here at my guesthouse in the middle of nowhere for weeks on end, and all you do every day is walk on the moors or wander about the village. Are you here for any particular reason?'

Slim shrugged. 'I'm a recovering alcoholic.'

'Yet you dine in the Crown every night?'

'Call it penance,' Slim said. 'I'm confronting my personal demons. Plus, I always sit in the family room, out of sight of the booze.'

'But why here? Why Penleven? If I hadn't noticed your inability to remember basic functions like to take your front door key when you go out, I might imagine you to be a spy in hiding.'

Slim shrugged. 'I couldn't afford to go abroad. And

I've always been attracted to Cornwall, particularly the cold, dark, featureless parts most people avoid.'

'Well, there's nowhere more like that than Penleven,' Mrs. Greyson said with an air of slight disappointment, as though she had once had an opportunity to leave but missed her chance. 'There are only a couple of hundred people in the village, but at least we're not a winter ghost town like many of the coastal villages.'

'Ghost town?'

'Boscastle, Port Isaac, Padstow … they're all holiday homes. Thriving in summer, deserted in winter. We might not be a bustling community, but at least there's always a friendly face in the shop or the pub.'

On the occasions he had ventured into the Crown's bar to order his meal, Slim had seen few friendly faces but lots of downtrodden ones, slumped over their pints, staring into space. Perhaps it was the winter—at night the wind howled, rattling his window hard enough, he feared sometimes, to rip it out of the wall, and it was proper dark on the road up to the guesthouse, not the city-dark Slim was accustomed to. Or perhaps it was that there was little to talk about in these parts. Slim got no reception on his phone unless he walked a mile uphill towards the A39, but for someone with more to forget than look forward to, it was an ideal situation.

As though giving up the hunt for the snippet of gossip that might briefly elevate her profile among the tongue-wagging older members of the community, Mrs. Greyson set Slim's breakfast down and stood back, folding her arms, standing watch for a few moments before abruptly turning on her heels and marching back into the kitchen. Slim was left alone in the guesthouse's cramped dining area: three tables pushed so tight against the walls they had marked the wallpaper, and one floating in the middle as though forgotten. Mrs. Greyson, in some act of defiance against his nerve at burdening her with his business, laid up the least desirable spot of all for Slim each morning, on a table tucked behind a door into the hall. The menu, with three of the four options crossed off, consisted only of a boiled cabbage fry up with an occasional side helping of baked beans. Slim had so much wind he had to leave his bedroom window open at night.

At least the toast was consistently pleasant, and the coffee, while lacking the extra something Slim might once have added, was strong and tasted like it was brewed yesterday, the way Slim liked it.

He finished up quickly, shouted thanks to Mrs. Greyson then headed out before she could corner him again. He was greeted by a damp wind whistling off Bodmin Moor a couple of miles to the east that challenged his jacket to keep him both dry and warm. Even when the moors were dry, Penleven was shrouded in the same mist-rain, as though owner of its own microcosmic weather system.

The bus was an acceptable ten minutes late, and took him on a seemingly endless meander through forested valleys along narrow, snaking lanes until finally emerging in the valley of the pretty town of Tavistock. Laid out along a stretch of the River Tavy, it was a pleasant collection of historic streets lined by surprisingly cosmopolitan shops. Enjoying the rare comfort of people, Slim took the opportunity to upgrade the old soap in Mrs. Greyson's bathroom, buy himself a t-shirt from H&M, and then took lunch in a Wetherspoons pub. Returning to his purpose after a big screen rugby game had finished, he located the indoor market near the river and asked around for an antiques dealer. Three people recommended Geoff Bunce, the owner of a bric-a-brac store tucked into the northeastern corner beside a bustling café.

'I need a clock valued,' Slim told the white-bearded Bunce, whose girth and facial hair gave him the appearance of an out-of-season Father Christmas, a look accentuated by the suspenders that stretched over his protruding belly.

'Let me take a look.'

Bunce turned the clock over several times, humming under his breath with contented appreciation, every so often glancing up at Slim with a suspicious narrowing of his eyes.

'You mind if I open up the back?'

'Sure.'

As Bunce got to work with a screwdriver, Slim took a seat beside his desk and let his eyes drift over the shelves and boxes loaded with bric-a-brac. Not so much antiques as dusty junk from pasts long forgotten.

'You a friend of old Birch?' Bunce said abruptly.

'What?'

Bunce held out a water-damaged envelope.

'Old Birch. Amos.'

Slim frowned, wondering if Bunce had slipped into a Cornish dialect. Then, with a hint of frustration, the man repeated, 'Amos Birch. The man who made this clock. Lived over in Trelee, near Bodmin Moor. Owned a farm. In his early days, used to sell his clocks right here in Tavistock market, before he got well-known. He was a friend of yours?'

'Yeah, a friend.'

'Then I'll guess this belongs to you.' The man shook the envelope as though to remind Slim of its existence.

Slim took it, immediately feeling the aged delicacy of the paper coupled with damp. If he tried to open it, the envelope would fall apart in his hands, and any message contained within would be lost.

'Ah, that's where that got to,' he said, giving the storekeeper an unconvincing grin. 'I was looking for that.'

'Sure you were, Mr.—?'

'Hardy. John Hardy, but people call me Slim.'

'I won't ask why.'

'Don't. It's not a story worth telling.'

Bunce sighed again. He turned the clock one more time. 'It's unfinished,' he said, confirming what Slim had already surmised. 'I'm guessing your friend Birch gave this to you as a gift? He couldn't have sold it in this condition, a man of his reputation.'

'It sounds like you knew him well.'

'School friends. Amos was two years older but there weren't a lot of kids around. Everyone knew everyone else.'

'I guess that's small communities for you.'

'You're not from round here, are you, Mr. Hardy?'

Slim had always felt he spoke with a neutral accent,

but that by itself made him an outsider where strong Westcountry accents were expected.

'Lancashire,' he said. 'But I spent a lot of time overseas.'

'Armed Forces?'

'How did you know?'

'Your eyes,' Bunce said. 'I see ghosts in them.'

Slim took a step back. A reel of unwanted memories began to flicker, which he shook off, shutting it down.

'You were in the Armed Forces too?'

'Falklands. Less said about that, the better.'

Slim nodded. At least they had some common ground. 'Well, I guess I've taken up too much of your time already—'

'You'd get a few hundred for it,' Bunce said, abruptly holding out the clock. 'Maybe a little more if you put it to auction. There are collectors out there for Amos Birch clocks, rare as they are. It's unfinished, and it's got some cosmetic damage, but it's still an Amos Birch original. They used to be sought after. Amos was a cottage industry before cottage industries were a thing.'

'Used to be?'

Bunce frowned, and Slim felt the man's eyes dissecting every thread of his lie.

'Interest in Amos Birch waned after he disappeared.'

'After he…?'

'You are aware, aren't you, Mr. Hardy, that your friend has been missing for over twenty years?'

5

THE CROWN & LION, THE LONELY PUB THAT SAT ON the very edge of Penleven, a screen of trees separating it from the nearest estate of houses like a shunned neighbour, had never looked more inviting. From the village's only bus stop Slim had no choice but to walk past it to reach the guesthouse, and while he had frequently dined in its tatty family room with little craving for the booze that would erase the last three months of recovery in the blink of a local's squinting eye, tonight he felt too much of the old tension, the nervous restlessness that had always pushed him over the edge. People said once an alcoholic, always an alcoholic, and while Slim had hopes of one day enjoying the occasional quiet beer, those demon-free days of control and contentment were a long way off. He gave the lights in the pub window a single longing glance, then quickened his step and hurried past.

The guesthouse was quiet when he returned, but

through a closed door came the muffled sound of a television with its volume turned down low. Slim cracked the door and saw Mrs. Greyson asleep in her chair in front of an electric fire. The television remote rested on the chair's arm beside her, as though she'd had the forethought to turn down the sound before nodding off.

Slim went upstairs. He put the clock on his bed then went back out. Half a mile down the road, outside the village's only shop, Slim found a payphone.

He called a friend back in Lancashire. Kay Skelton was a linguistics and translation expert whom Slim knew from his Armed Forces days, and with whom he had worked before. Slim explained about the old letter found in the back of the clock.

'I need to know what's written on it, if anything,' Slim said.

'Mail it to me special delivery,' Kay said. 'It's not something I can do, but I have a friend who can help.'

After ending the call, Slim was surprised to find the shop still open, even at nearly six fifteen.

'I'm just closing,' came the stern greeting from the shopkeeper, an elderly woman with a face so sour Slim doubted she could smile if she tried.

'I'll only be a minute,' Slim said.

'Ah, they all say that, don't they?' she said with a grin and a sarcastic laugh which left Slim unsure whether she were making a joke or being rude.

After buying an envelope Slim learned that, yes, the shop also functioned as a local post office, but while yes, it could arrange special delivery mail, a surcharge was required for out-of-hours mailing.

'Is it far from here to Trelee?' he asked, as the shopkeeper not so subtly herded him toward the door.

'Why'd you want to go up there? Not much up there for tourists.'

'I heard there's something of a mystery to the place.'

The shopkeeper rolled her eyes. 'Ah, you mean Amos Birch, the clockmaker. I thought that was old news by now. What do you care about an old man going missing?'

'I'm a private investigator. The story caught my interest.'

'Why? There's very little to tell. Did someone hire you?'

So much disdain was placed on the word 'hire' that Slim wondered if the shopkeeper had had a bad experience with PIs in the past.

'I'm on holiday,' he said. 'But you know what they say—once a cop, always a cop.'

'Do they say that, do they?'

'So … left or right out of the village?'

The shopkeeper rolled her eyes again. 'North on the old Camelford road. You might see a sign—there used to be one, but the council doesn't cut the weeds back like it used to. About ten minutes by car.'

'On foot?'

'An hour. A bit more, perhaps. If you know the way you can cut across the edge of Bodmin Moor and save some time, but be careful. It used to be mining country.'

'Thanks.'

'And take something to eat. This here's the only shop

from here until you reach the Shell garage on the A39 just outside Camelford.'

Slim nodded. 'Thanks for the information.'

The shopkeeper shrugged. 'If you want my advice, I'd save myself the effort. Not much to see but an old farmhouse, and not much to know. When Amos Birch disappeared, he made sure he'd never be found.'

6

R<small>AIN GREETED</small> S<small>LIM THE NEXT MORNING, BUT</small> M<small>RS.</small> Greyson was in as cheery a mood as he'd ever seen her when he explained he was going out.

'Not the best day for the moors, is it?' she said. When Slim shrugged, she added, 'I mean, I do have an umbrella I could lend you, but you can hardly use it on your push bike, and in any case, the wind up there will play havoc with it.'

Slim considered calling her bluff and requesting it anyway, but decided to take his chances with his regular jacket. Mrs. Greyson did offer him an old Ordnance Survey map, however, with Trelee marked as an enlarged dot a couple of grid squares above where Penleven was granted rather more space than its sparse cluster of houses deserved.

The road was as he'd come to expect of Cornwall anywhere away from the A30 or A39: an endless meandering lane barely wide enough for two vehicles to pass, a tangle of blind corners and hidden junctions dipping into and out of wooded valleys between rolling hills of farmland and moor. Claustrophobic hedgerows occasionally opened out to reveal ruggedly beautiful panoramas of misty open space, but walking through the gloom cast by overhanging trees, with his only companion the distant barking of a dog or the cry of a bird, Slim's imagination began to taunt him with images of mangled bodies and missing persons' advertisements in the back of Sunday newspapers.

Trelee, at the chink in the road where the map indicated the village should be, was barely a dozen houses, spaced out along half a mile of a flatter stretch broken by gateways into open fields carrying views across to Bodmin Moor. A few farm lanes disappeared into hidden valleys, clusters of secluded barns and farmhouses revealing only rooftops through leafless trees.

Slim chained his bike to a gate near to a council sign announcing TRELEE in confident lettering, the grass around it hacked down as though beaten by a stick, then continued on foot, wondering if he'd wasted a journey. The three nearest houses were modern bungalows set back from the road. None had vehicles outside, suggesting the occupants were off at work in some faraway metropolis. He spotted a few other signs of life: a scattering of children's toys on the driveway of one, an elegant cat sitting in the window of another.

Past the bungalows were three older cottages, stonewalled and thatch-roofed, a slice of travel documentary transported into Cornwall's nowhere. The first two looked empty, gates bolted and postboxes taped over, but an old man pottered in the garden of the third, emptying the skeletal remnants of dead plants onto a compost heap before stacking the old trays into a pile.

Slim lifted a hand in response to a polite greeting.

'I wondered if you could spare a minute?' he called.

The man wandered over. 'Sure. Are you new round here?'

'Just visiting. Holiday.'

The man gave a thoughtful nod. 'Nice. I would have picked somewhere a little closer to the coast, but each to their own.'

Slim shrugged. 'It was cheap.'

'No surprise there.'

'I'm looking for someone who might have known Amos Birch,' Slim said, the words out before he really knew what he was saying. 'I'm aware that he's passed, but I wondered if he perhaps had a wife or a son. I found something that might belong to him.'

The man visibly tensed at Amos's name. 'Whether he's passed or not is a matter of debate. Who wants to know?'

'My name's Slim Hardy. I'm staying at the Lakeview Guesthouse in Penleven.'

'And what did you find?'

Slim figured there was no point holding anything back. 'A clock. I heard he was a bit of a hobbyist.'

The man laughed. 'A hobbyist? Who told you that?'

'Just what I heard.'

'Well, my friend, if you happened to find an Amos

Birch clock I'd keep it to myself, or at least under lock and key.'

'Why is that?'

'Those things are highly sought after. Amos Birch was no hobbyist. He was a nationally renowned artisan. His clocks are worth thousands.'

7

As Slim sat across a rickety table from the old man who had introduced himself as Lester 'but call me Les' Coates, he found himself constantly thinking about the clock he had casually left on his bed in the guesthouse. It might be worth a small fortune, something that, in the absence of any upcoming work, would be handy right now.

'The stories, they went on and on,' Les said over tea that Slim found frustratingly weak. 'It was literally a case of here today, gone tomorrow. Everything from falling down a mine shaft on Bodmin Moor to a kidnapping by an international terrorist group. Quite fanciful, you might say.'

'He lived near here?'

'At Worth Farm. Head north from mine, the second entrance on the left. He had hands who worked the farm for him, but it was a minimal operation. People always claimed he ran it at a loss as a tax break.'

'For his clocks?'

'Later on. He started out as a farmer, took the farm over from his father, I believe. Then, when interest in his side work grew, he cut back on one to expand on the other.'

'Were you friends?'

Les shook his head. 'Neighbours. Weren't no one really Old Birch's friend. Wasn't the most sociable of people but he was friendly enough if you saw him in the street.'

'Family?'

'Wife and a daughter. Mary survived him for a few years, but after she passed Celia sold the place and moved away. New couple in there is the Tinton's. Nice enough people, keep themselves to themselves. Maggie's a bit posh, but she's all right.'

'Did they know the history of the place when they bought it?'

Les shook his head. 'I wouldn't know. I didn't even know Celia had it up for sale until removal vans started showing up. Certainly weren't no sale signs up until the sold one appeared. Would have been nice to see a local buy it, but you can't help these things. No one was sad to see Celia go, though. Good riddance.'

Slim frowned at the abrupt change in Les's tone. It reminded him of the reaction he had first received on mentioning Amos. 'Why do you say that?'

Les sighed. 'Girl was a bad seed. Old Birch, he had money. Girl didn't want for nothing. Ran around like nobody's business. All sorts of things got said about her.'

'Like what?'

Les looked pained, grimacing as though the words were a fruit rotten on the inside that he had no choice but to swallow.

'She liked her men, so they said. Preferred them married. More than a couple of houses got sold while she was around, families going their separate ways. She was only nineteen when Amos disappeared, and there were plenty who said he'd had enough.'

'Do you think she killed him?'

Les slapped the table hard enough to make Slim jerk back, then let out a barking laugh. 'Oh God, no. You think she'd get away with something like that? Girl had her skills, but couldn't think her way out of a paper bag.'

Slim wanted to ask if Les knew Celia's new address, but the old man was frowning as he stared off into space. Slim glanced around, looking for signs of a woman's presence and found none. He wondered if the tales of Celia Birch's decadent lifestyle were coming from more than just hearsay.

'Thanks for your time,' he said, standing up. 'I'll let you be about your day.'

Les led Slim to the door. 'Come around anytime,' he said. 'But if you want my advice? Don't dig too deep.'

'What do you mean?'

'Doors around here are always open for a stranger. But if you pry too much into what goes on behind, they tend to slam closed.'

8

Slim ate lunch beside a stile overlooking the distant green baize of Bodmin Moor. Footprints in the soft mud at the field's corner told him the route was a popular one, but he'd seen no other walkers yet.

He felt a little uncomfortable knocking on the door of Worth Farm, but the footpath down into the valley angled around the back of the farmyard before cutting across a stream and heading onto the moor, so Slim could look through the hedgerow as he passed.

A farmhouse fronted a concrete yard encircled by outbuildings: two large barns for animals, one for machinery, and a couple of others whose uses Slim could only guess at; grain silos or a dairy, perhaps. At the back of the main courtyard, a gravel path led down to a cluster of smaller outhouses that had the feel of personal use about them. Slim squinted through the fence, wondering if the largest of them—a brick shed with two windows either side of a door, and a small chimney protruding from the roof at one end—had once been Amos Birch's workshop.

With an instinct for possible clues developed over eight years as a private investigator, Slim pulled out his digital camera and took a few shots of the farmyard. He had slipped it back into his pocket just a moment before a woman's voice hailed him.

'You know, you could get stuck up there.'

Slim jerked, twisting around. He slid out of the hedge to land in a heap in the mud at the bottom. As he turned, grimacing at the brown smear reaching from his ankle halfway up his thigh, he found himself face to face with an elderly lady decked out in tweed hiking garb. She leaned on a walking stick and peered up at him, eyes squinting through spectacles that sat low on her nose.

Slim climbed to his feet and wiped the mud off his clothes as best he could. The woman continued to watch him, frown deepening, head cocked to one side like an auteur examining a rival artwork.

'Did you spot anything of interest from your vantage point?'

'What?'

'From your spot in that thicket.' She waved her walking stick towards the moor. 'You know, most people on this path are looking over yonder, up at those spectacular tors. I wondered what you could possibly find so interesting about a few farm buildings hidden away behind a hedge pruned in such a way that someone with even a shred of intelligence might ascertain as an attempt at privacy?'

The woman's tone had turned from general interest to one bordering on anger. Slim was tiring of her airs and graces, but it suddenly dawned on him who he was talking with.

'Mrs. Tinton? You own Worth Farm, don't you?'

The woman gave a sharp nod. 'Clever, aren't you? I do indeed. And I'll tell you something: I don't care who used to live here. I'm sick of you treasure hunter-types snooping around. I've been telling Trevor for years that the erection of an electric fence is the only way to go, but he always thinks each Peeping Tom we catch sniffing around our property will be the last. Honestly, sometimes he's too kind for his own good.'

'I'm sorry.'

'And so you should be. Now, you get away from that hedgerow at once. The right to roam might protect you on the path, but that hedgerow is part of my property, and by climbing it you're committing a trespass. You do know you can be fined up to five thousand pounds for trespassing, don't you?'

In a moment of urgency related to a prior case, Slim had once trawled through a beginners' guide to Britain's laws and remembered no such thing, but calling her on it would achieve nothing. He spread his hands, gave her his most apologetic smile and said, 'I didn't mean any harm.'

'Worth Farm is not a tourist attraction!'

The woman stabbed her walking stick into the ground for emphasis, splashing mud over Slim's already-soaked boots. He considered another protest, but decided not to bother. She hadn't noticed the camera, so it was best to get away while he could.

'I'd better be getting home,' he said, backing away down the path while she shook her stick at him. 'Again, I apologise. I didn't mean any harm.'

'Get away with you!'

Slim stumbled away down the path. Once among the trees at the bottom of the field he risked a glance back. Mrs. Tinton had walked up the path to the stile, but there she had resumed her sentry duty, leaning on the walking stick with both hands like a soldier with a rifle.

Only the longer route around the back of the farm would take him back to the road without passing her. The path followed a narrow, treacherous riverbank with a steep drop into the stream. The tall hedgerow bordering the farm offered only handfuls of brambles to support him, while a line of trees planted on the farm side laid a confusing web of shadows on the uneven ground. In places the stream had washed away part of the path, and one section of the hedge near the southeastern corner was supported by a newer stone wall, suggesting it had once been undercut and collapsed.

The first spots of rain began to patter around him as the path opened out into another field. From inside a quaint conservatory with a plate of scones or even a bottle of whisky in front of him, it would have been a welcome, romantic sound. Now, though, it reminded Slim of the long bike ride back to Penleven. He wondered if it wasn't about time to ditch Cornwall and head back up country, but he couldn't face the hassle of flat hunting or the temptations that the stress might bring. Instead, he glowered at the murky sky, and stepped out of the last cover of the trees into the rain.

On returning to the guesthouse an hour later, Mrs. Greyson berated him for getting mud on the doormat, but otherwise seemed pleased to see him back before dark. In his room he snacked on crisps and chocolate while uploading his pictures to his laptop. He didn't expect to find much of note, but when he enlarged the image of the small brick building, a couple of things caught his eye.

Inside the windows to either side there appeared to be bars, while the door was adorned by a heavy padlock.

9

Amos Birch's disappearance had proven too uneventful to cause much stir on the internet. Through some extensive trawling and a little bit of sorting the fan sites and speculation from the reputable sources, Slim was able to determine the exact date as the second of May, 1996, a Thursday, twenty-one years and ten months ago. According to historical weather reports, it had been cloudy in the morning, with a light drizzle from around four o'clock onwards.

The only detailed article related to the disappearance itself was on a blog for clock enthusiasts, a where-are-they-now post about amateur clockmakers which covered little that Slim didn't already know. On the night of Thursday, May 2nd, 1996, Amos Birch had eaten dinner with his wife and daughter, then retired to his workshop to continue working on his latest clock. He was never seen again.

Speculation ranged from murder to elopement. He

was fifty-three years old at the time, and shared the family home with his wife, Mary, then 47, and daughter, Celia, 19. A police investigation took place, involving an extensive search of Bodmin Moor, but came to the conclusion, in the absence of evidence to suggest otherwise, that Amos Birch had simply got up and walked away from his life. The workshop was left unlocked, and only his walking boots and jacket were missing. He had taken no identification with him, and his wallet was later found in a kitchen drawer. However, since it was believed that he sold a lot of his clocks cash-in-hand to local collectors, the absence of any ATM withdrawals in the days afterwards meant that he most likely ran with cash on him, later setting up a new identity.

The article had no other details of note, but the last line struck a chord with Slim.

It appeared that Birch had simply got up and walked out the door, taking his last clock with him.

There was nothing to suggest the author knew about the clock. Nowhere else was there mention of a clock left unfinished in the workshop, so it could have been a line of fanciful imagination.

Was the last clock the one Slim found out on the moor?

Geoff Bunce had agreed with Slim's assessment that the clock was unfinished. What if Amos Birch's last clock now lay under Slim's bed?

Slim stood up, feeling suddenly nervous. He paced the room a few times. There was no knowing the circumstances of Amos's disappearance, but Slim had not been quiet about what he had found. What if Amos had hidden the clock for a specific reason?

What if someone was after it? Could Amos have disappeared, taking the clock with him, to hide it from someone?

Slim took the chair from under the room's little desk, then tilted and lodged it under the door handle. He hadn't considered the absence of a lock to be a problem, but it couldn't hurt him to be cautious.

He wondered if he ought to say something to Mrs. Greyson, but thought better of it. He was only likely to worry her, and in any case, he would be the person sought after, not her.

Unless of course, Amos had been murdered. Bodmin Moor and the surrounding area had allegedly been heavily mined in the past, and the ground was dotted with old shafts, many of which were not mapped or identified. How hard would it have been to dispose of Amos's body where no one would ever find it?

10

AT BREAKFAST THE NEXT MORNING, SLIM JUDGED THAT Mrs. Greyson was in a good mood, so he called her over. At his request, the whistling that had drifted from the kitchen like the song of an aging but joyful bird abruptly died, and she stomped over, wringing her apron as though to remind Slim of the inconvenience he had dared to cause.

'Mr. Hardy … I trust everything is to your liking?'

He smiled, prodding the plate with a fork. 'Of course. These eggs remind me of my long-dead mother and the culinary delights I was subjected to on a daily basis.'

'That's … good. How can I help you today?'

'Yesterday I went up to Trelee. I got a little lost on the moor, but an old lady was kind enough to offer me directions. I wanted to send her a note of thanks, but I'm afraid I forgot her name.'

'And how do you think I would know it?'

'She said she lived at Amos Birch's old place. Worth Farm. I don't suppose you know the name of the new owners?'

'Hardly new; they've been in there a dozen years.'

Slim held his smile, but nodded as though to encourage further comment.

'Tinton,' Mrs. Greyson said. 'Maggie Tinton. I can only say you must have caught her on a good day. As sour an old crone as you'll find round here. And I bet you were thinking I was bad.'

Slim's smile was starting to make his face ache.

'Her husband, Trevor, he's far more pleasant. Used to drink in the Crown until the … well, that was a while back.'

'Until what?'

Mrs. Greyson unrolled her apron, snapped it out and then frowned as though Slim was asking her to cross a moral line.

'There was talk … people said they'd had a hand in it.'

'In what?'

'In Amos's disappearance.' Before Slim could respond, she added, 'Which is ridiculous, of course. The Tintons come from London. They can't have known anything about Amos. After all, Mary was living there for a decade after Amos disappeared. The Tintons just spotted a bargain.'

'Do people really think they had something to do with it?'

'Of course not. It was just a silly rumour, but they

both took offence, and after that, they isolated themselves from the local community.'

'It sounds like you know them well.'

'I used to play bridge at the legion hall with Maggie, but she stopped coming and never came back.'

'It's almost like an admission of guilt.'

'They were affronted, that's all,' she said. 'They moved here to retire into the archetypal country life you see on television. I think they envisaged a community of local simpletons waiting with open arms to take them to village fêtes and coffee mornings. When they didn't get what they wanted they gave up.'

'But there's no way they had anything to do with Amos Birch's disappearance?'

Mrs. Greyson shook her head. 'Absolutely none.'

'So what do you think happened?'

Mrs. Greyson rolled her eyes. 'I thought we were talking about Mrs. Tinton?'

'You must wonder. It sounds like you knew them quite well.'

Mrs. Greyson shrugged and sighed. 'He ran out on his family. What is there to know? Amos had plenty of money tucked away, and he was often off on his business trips, clock conventions and all that. You want my opinion? He had some floosy overseas and he ran off to be with her.'

'Wouldn't it have been easier for him to just divorce Mary?'

Mrs. Greyson wrang her apron again. 'I don't have time for this,' she said, giving a little shake of the head.

As she turned and headed for the kitchen, she added, 'Enjoy your walk today, Mr. Hardy.'

Slim stared after her, frowning. He would get no more out of her, he felt sure, but on mention of another woman, her cheeks had taken on a reddish hue that definitely hadn't been there before.

11

To visit the nearest local library meant a return to Tavistock. Slim found himself alone in an archives room, poring over enormous files of old broadsheet local newspapers, browned and crisped by age.

Each file contained a year's worth of weeklies. As he had expected of small-town newspapers dominated by ads for local estate agents and farm machinery rental firms, there was little sensationalism about the brief reports on Amos Birch's disappearance. *Local clockmaker disappears in mysterious circumstances* read the title of one, before continuing with a report so bland it was almost an oxymoron of its title, focusing on Amos's background as an artisan of rare skill and a well-respected local farmer, but leaving out any trace of speculation.

He found the most interesting report in a file for a newspaper called the Tavistock Tribune:

· · ·

"Local farmer and renowned clockmaker, Amos Birch (53), has been missing since the evening of Thursday, May 2nd, it has been reported to police by his wife, Mary (47). Well-known both domestically and internationally for his intricate, handmade timepieces, it is believed that Amos may have taken an evening stroll across Bodmin Moor and become lost. He was considered to be in sound mind and had no health issues, but, according to his wife, had become increasingly agitated in the week leading up to his disappearance. The family requests that any information regarding Amos's disappearance be passed to Devon & Cornwall Police."

Slim read the article over a couple of times, then frowned. Agitated? It could mean anything, but it suggested Amos was aware something might be about to happen. Did it mean he had planned to run away, or did something happen to him?

Remembering a quote an old army colleague had told him about how the clues to a crime were often laid long before the crime itself, he cycled back a few weeks, scanning over the news pages for anything at all relating to Amos Birch. Barring a two-inch column over a month before the disappearance which recognised a national clockmaker's association accolade awarded to Amos, there was nothing.

By lunchtime, his eyes ached from staring at age-blurred print, so he relocated to a nearby coffee shop to recuperate. There he called Kay, but his translator friend had no information yet on the contents of the letter.

The mind he had turned to private investigation a

few years after his dishonorable discharge from the Armed Forces was beginning to whir with fanciful ideas. No one got up and left a stable relationship without reason. You were either running to something, or from something.

The possibilities were endless. A lover was the obvious to, a disgruntled client or a competitor the obvious from. Without much of a picture of Amos himself, it was hard to make judgements. From Slim's conversations so far, the clockmaker had been a shadowy figure in the community, the very obscurity of his profession bringing with it a label of mystery. Even the lane down to Worth Farm and the high hedgerows surrounding it gave the Birch family an air of seclusion, one that the Tintons had continued.

The café had a payphone. Slim took a phonebook from a shelf beside it and returned to his table. There were a couple of dozen Birches listed, but none with a C.

Slim was walking back to the bus station when he heard someone shout behind him. Something in its urgency made him turn, and he found Geoff Bunce waving at him from the other side of the street. Slim waited while the man crossed.

'I thought it was you. A long holiday you're on.'

Slim shrugged. 'I'm self-employed. I take as long as I like.'

'Did you meet him, then? Your friend?'

The sarcasm in the man's tone caused a ripple of anger in Slim's stomach, but he forced a casualness into his voice. 'Amos Birch?'

'Yeah. Gave his clock back to him, did you?'

'Not yet. It's a work in progress.'

'Look, I don't know who you are, but I think it might be wise for you to take that clock and go back to where you came from.'

Slim couldn't help but smile. He was an ex-marine who'd served time for ABH being threatened by Santa Claus in a green wax jacket. Bunce might have claimed to be ex-Armed Forces, but it was difficult to see it.

'What's so funny?'

'Nothing. I'm just intrigued by the sharpness of your tone. I'm just a man looking to sell an old clock.'

'Now, you see, Mr. Hardy, that's the last thing I think you are.'

'You remembered my name.'

'I wrote it down. Something about you didn't feel right.'

'Just something?' Slim sighed, tiring of the games. 'Look, you want the truth? I'm down here on holiday. I found that clock buried out on Bodmin Moor. The damn thing nearly broke my ankle. It just so happens that my current day job—for better or worse—is as a private investigator. It's hard to resist a mystery.'

Bunce wrinkled his nose. 'Well, that changes things.'

'What do you mean?'

The other man nodded, then puffed out his cheeks, as though preparing to reveal some major revelation. Slim lifted an eyebrow.

'You see,' Bunce said, 'I was the last person—outside the immediate family—to see Amos Birch alive.'

12

'So, where is it now, that clock you found?'

Slim sat across from Geoff Bunce in a café on the corner of Tavistock market. He sipped weak coffee out of a Styrofoam cup and said, 'I hid it.'

'Where?'

Slim smiled. 'Somewhere I'm sure it'll be safe.'

Bunce nodded quickly. 'Right, right. Good idea. So, do you have any idea what happened to Amos?'

'None whatsoever.'

'But you're a private investigator, right?'

'I deal mostly with extra-marital affairs and disability frauds,' Slim said. 'Nothing too exciting. I'm not making any money off this investigation, so when the trail runs cold I'll likely disappear back up country and find a case that pays.'

'Don't you have any clues?'

'What I have is a mental list of possibilities, and the more I can cross off, the closer I'll get to figuring out what really happened.'

'What do you have on your list?'

Slim laughed. 'Pretty much everything from murder to alien abduction.'

'You don't really think—' Bunce cut off abruptly, his nose wrinkling. 'Ah, a joke. I see.'

'I really have no clue. At the moment I'm just trying to establish the circumstances surrounding his disappearance. Perhaps you can help me with that.'

'In what way?'

'You said you were the last person to see him alive outside his family. How about you tell me about that?'

Bunce shrugged, looking suddenly uncertain. 'Well, it was a long time ago now, wasn't it? We went for a walk on the moors, up to Yarrow Tor, past the abandoned farmhouse over there.'

'Do you remember why?'

Bunce shrugged one shoulder in a strange, lopsided gesture. 'It was a usual route. We did it every couple of months. No special reason.'

'Do you remember what you talked about?'

Bunce shook his head. 'Ah … it would have been the usual stuff. We weren't much for deep conversations. We saw each other a lot, you know. It was always gripes about the weather, the odd complaint about politics, that kind of thing.'

'You're not giving me much to go on.'

Bunce looked disappointed. 'I suppose there's not much to say. I mean, I'd known Amos forever, but we weren't the kind of close where we'd tell each other everything. He wasn't that kind of man.

People often joked that he preferred clocks to people.'

'You told me that clock was worth a few hundred quid. How good was he, really?'

Bunce smiled, appearing relieved that Slim had asked a question he could answer.

'He was like a mathematician with his hands. Most craftsmen have one particular skill, but Amos was a complete package. He did all the designing, the carvings, as well as built all the mechanical internal workings by hand. Do you have any idea how hard it is to fashion clock parts by hand? A day's work will make you one or two small parts. It's labour- intensive, and few people these days have that kind of concentration. He was a rare breed, was Amos.'

'How many did he make?'

'Not all that many. Two or three a year. Some were commissions, I believe, others private sales. He wasn't in a hurry. He had no desire to be rich. He liked his moors, liked the quiet life. His farm turned a small profit— despite what many people say—and the sale of his clocks brought in enough extra to give him that little level of luxury.'

'Was it likely someone could have held a grudge toward him? Perhaps a failed sale, or a deal gone wrong?'

'Possible, but I'd doubt it. Amos was a humbly likable man.'

'How do you mean?'

Bunce gave his beard a tug. 'He was inoffensive, that's the best way I could put it. He was quietly spoken, and never had a bad word to say about anyone. He buried himself in his work. And his work was good. Who could complain about clocks made with such love and care. I mean, how often do cuckoo clocks break? How many times have you walked into a pub and seen a broken one on the wall in a corner? Amos's clocks, though … I mean, how long was that clock buried? Twenty years? And yet you can wind it straight up and have it working again just like that? No clock you buy in a shop will have that kind of durability. Built to last, Amos's clocks were.'

Bunce had nothing more of interest to say, so Slim took his number, made his excuses, and left. He had reached the bus station and was standing in line for a ticket when a thought struck him.

He took out Bunce's number and called the antiques dealer.

'Need me again so soon?'

Slim smiled. 'I just had a quick question. With a clock like the one I found, how often would you suggest winding it?'

'Oh, I don't know, once every few months. Amos used to make these incredible springs. You could wind them and they'd last for ages.'

'Okay, thanks.'

When he got back to the guesthouse, Mrs. Greyson was dusting in the hall. Slim gave her a polite good evening, then hurried up to his room. There, he pulled out the clock from under the bed and sat listening to the ticking for a few minutes. Then he turned it over, removed the wooden panel Bunce had left unscrewed, and looked at the clock mechanism. The small dial which wound the clock was reverberating slightly with each tick.

He frowned, touching it lightly with a finger, noticing the lack of grime compared to the rest of the clock.

Every few months, Bunce had said. If the clock had been buried for twenty odd years, the spring would have wound down long ago.

Slim hadn't wound it, which left him with the question: who had?

13

SOMEONE KNEW THE LOCATION OF THE BURIED CLOCK, and cared enough about it to return every few months to wind it. Such an action required a reason. Sentimentality was one, but that took the most effort, something likely to wane over time. Who could possibly want the clock to continue running, and why? As Slim turned it over, his mind was blank. Ornate, yes, but it was just a clock. Sure, the cuckoo mechanism made an appreciable noise, but nothing that could be heard from underground. Slim had thought it broken until the little wooden bird had burst out of its box to surprise him.

Slim replaced the clock under his bed, slipped on his jacket and headed out into the night. It was time to step into the closest thing Penleven had to a bear pit in search of further information—the Crown. Drinkers liked to talk, but if Amos Birch still had enemies, there Slim would likely find them.

He took a deep breath and pushed through the

doors. A clock over the bar said half past nine. Four faces turned toward him. An old man perched on a stool, his face a wrinkled dishcloth surrounded by rebelling white hair. Two men playing cards at a table near a crackling fire: one wiry thin and hollow-eyed, as though he considered food a mortal enemy, the other hard-faced and thick with builder's muscle. Tattoos poked below the hem of a t-shirt straining against knotted biceps as he glared at a pair of sevens before pushing a handful of coins across the table.

'Pint?'

The fourth person, a woman Slim would kindly consider muscular, unkindly as dumpy, watched him from behind the bar. An unbuttoned blouse revealed a triangle of cleavage optimistic enough to deflect attention from her face, where overlarge eyebrows and a slightly sour set of her lips killed off any last possibility of attractiveness.

Slim hesitated, his eyes locked on the glass held at a tilt toward the nearest beer tap. So easy to undo so much work. With a knot in his stomach, he said, 'I'm driving,' in a timid voice that felt unfamiliar.

'I didn't hear your car come in.'

She had tilted her head away from the glass. Her bosom gave a little tremble, and Slim forced himself not to look. She was the wrong side of forty, but probably less wrong than he.

'Tomorrow,' he muttered.

She nodded. 'We've got free on tap. That do? Probably near its sell-by, but it tastes like piss anyway.'

'That'll be fine.'

Slim took a stool by the bar, leaving an empty spot between himself and the old man. The two men playing cards were behind him, their outlines reflected in a glass wine cabinet behind the bar.

'You's the lad eats in the family room,' the old man said. 'You shy? Ain't no one be afraid of in here.'

Slim was just preparing a reply when the woman said, 'He's the one been asking about old Amos.'

Before Slim could answer, she added, 'We don't get much to talk about in a place like this. You're the biggest gossip practically since he ran off.'

She thumped a frothing pint on the bar mat nearest to him. Slim eyed it with suspicion. Non-alcoholic, it might be, but it looked remarkably like the real thing.

'Nah, there was Mary's passing, then there was Celia, then—'

'All right, Reg, was a figure of speech.'

'I like a good mystery,' Slim said.

'Heard you was a private eye,' the woman said. 'Got your eye on anyone?' She winked then burst into horsey laughter, slapping the edge of the bar with one hand.

'June's husband left her,' Reg said. 'I'd watch out. She'll take anyone.'

'You can forget it!' June said. Then, to Slim, she added, 'Don't listen to him. No idea what's going on half the time.'

Slim smiled as he let the banter run on a while. It was quickly apparent that Reg was a regular, the kind of ever-present who kept a pub running during the long, dark winter. After half an hour, a middle-aged couple entered, took a table at the far end of the bar and made a food order which kept June busy for a while. Slim sipped his metal-tasting pint of beer-flavoured water, nodding as Reg spun tales of country life so easily forgettable that when Reg started on another about a broken-down tractor, Slim was sure had heard it before.

Eventually, as he had hoped, conversation came back around to Amos Birch.

'You know, I was a bit younger, but we both went to the same primary. They had one up in Boswinnick, but it's gone now. Went to Liskeard Secondary but Birch never went there. Some said he was a bit odd, you know, but back then you didn't have to go school all that long. His father ran Worth Farm, needed his help. When the old man died, farm was his. Caused many a scowl when Celia sold it. Said you could find Birches at Worth Farm back in the Domesday Book. Sold out their legacy, that girl did.'

'Why?'

Reg sighed. 'Ah, who knows? Girl wasn't much liked round here, for one reason or another. Didn't really fit the scene, you city folk might say.'

Slim had more questions, but Reg downed the last quarter of his drink and stood up.

'Well, that's me done. Goodnight to you.'

Slim watched him walk out. Behind him, the two men continued their card game. June returned from serving food and looked surprised to see Reg gone.

'He just left,' Slim said.

June frowned. She was about to speak when a chair scraped and the tattooed man stood up. Slim listened to his footsteps as he made his way to the bar, Slim's Armed Forces sixth sense detecting tension, a threat.

He didn't move as the man leaned close. Warm ale breath tickled his ear.

'You want to watch about asking too many questions,' the man said. 'Some folk might be happy to talk, but others might prefer the past to stay where it is.'

'Michael, that's enough,' June said in a low voice.

Slim tensed. His army muscles had softened in the eighteen years since his dishonourable discharge, but he still knew a trick or two if it came to a fight. He waited to see what would happen. Michael maintained his threatening pose a few moments longer, then turned and stalked back to his table.

Slim sipped what remained of his pint, then stood up. 'I think I'll be going,' he said.

June gave him a sorry look then wished him goodnight.

Outside, a gale had got up, ragging the hedgerows, throwing squalls of rain out of the dark that raked at Slim's face before retreating like a lunging animal. Slim pulled his jacket up around his neck and hunched down, wondering, if anything, what he had gained from his pub visit.

The lights of the guesthouse had appeared through a stand of trees when Slim paused. A regular tapping sound came over the top of the wind.

Running feet.

Slim cursed his slow reactions. The newcomer was too close for him to take cover; his silhouette would be visible against the grey sky to someone with eyes adjusted to the dark.

He turned, bringing his fists up, waiting for Michael's attack, hoping the man hadn't had time to find a weapon.

A woman's gasp came from a feminine shape stumbling to a halt behind him.

'Slim?'

'June?'

Her hand touched his shoulder. 'Slim, I can't be long. I have to hurry back. They think I'm in the kitchens. I just wanted to say sorry for Michael.'

'I've suffered worse.'

'He's not normally like that. It's just that … he was with Celia. You know, back then.'

'Back when?'

'When Amos disappeared. Michael was Celia's boyfriend at the time.'

'And what does that matter?'

'Amos's disappearance … they were engaged at the time, but afterwards she broke it off, and he's never gotten over it.'

14

S<small>LIM DIDN'T SLEEP WELL, TOSSING AND TURNING AS</small> images of knives flashing out of the dark kept him waking up through the early hours.

After saying good morning to Mrs. Greyson, he walked up the road to the end of the village, then up a winding lane to a hilltop with a view across Penleven. There he was able to pick up a faint mobile phone signal.

After a couple of minutes his phone buzzed, updating with a missed call from Kay. Slim called back.

'Kay. What do you have for me?'

'I won't ask what you're mixed up in this time, Slim.'

'Was there a message on the paper?'

'Yes.' Kay cleared his throat. '"*Charlotte, your time is forever. I will wait for you, always.*" There's a second line too, but it's nearly illegible. In fact, I'm not sure it's anything at all. There are a series of dashes which could be simple underlines. There's a word near the beginning that looks like "amser". In the middle, there's a word which looks like "puppy", but that's it. At the end there's an initial I can't quite make out because the paper is slightly damaged. It looks like an A.'

Slim closed his eyes and nodded. 'Nice work. Anything else you can give me?'

'I'll scan everything and send it down to you by next post. I want to keep the original for a while, if that's okay. I have a friend who works in forensics who might be able to tell us something about the paper. And it's handwritten, of course. You could perhaps identify it if you took samples from suspects.'

Slim thanked Kay and hung off. He was buzzing with excitement, almost enough to send him back to the Crown to celebrate. *Don't go there,* he reminded himself. The clear mind of sobriety was proving quite useful.

Instead of answers, he just had more questions, and one was prominent above the others.

Who was Charlotte?

15

'MICHAEL? MICHAEL POLSON, YOU MEAN? YES, I know him. Comes into the shop from time to time.' The shopkeeper, whose name Slim had now learned was Mrs. Waite, returned to packing Slim's bag. 'Anything else, Mr… um….'

'Hardy.'

'Mr. Hardy?'

'That's all for now. Do you know where I could find Michael?'

'The pub, I'd expect. He's a bit rough around the edges, if you know what I mean.'

'Yes, I know. Outside the pub, where could I find him?'

'Oh, I see. Well, I think your best bet is over at Lodge, on the edge of the moor. He used to work at Worth Farm but moved over to Lodge after Amos disappeared.'

'Lodge?'

'Lodge Farm. It's owned by Peter Entwhistle, although he's too old to be seen out much these days.'

'Thank you.'

'Can I ask why you're after him?'

Slim smiled. Behind her eyes he could see the gossip motors warming up. It wasn't unlikely that Mrs Greyson would know of his business before he returned.

'Oh, it's nothing much important,' he said. 'I'll just catch up with him when I get a chance. I'm sorry, but I have a shocking sense of direction. Could I trouble you to write down directions to Lodge Farm?'

'Well, sure.'

Mrs. Waite tore a sheet of note paper off a pad and scribbled down a few lines, complete with a crude map.

'Thanks, that's very kind of you.' Slim took it from her, gave it a passing glance, then folded it neatly and slipped it into a pocket.

'Thanks for your help,' he said, heading for the door. He paused with it half open and turned back. 'I don't suppose you know anyone called Charlotte?' he asked.

Mrs. Waite frowned. 'I don't recall anyone by that name.'

'Someone who used to live around here?'

Mrs. Waite shook her head. 'I'm afraid not.'

'Not to worry.'

He headed back to the guesthouse. The door was unlocked as it usually was during the day, so he let himself in, calling out Mrs. Greyson's name. From the living room came the light buzz of the TV, the inane exclamations of a cooking show.

Slim gave the door a light tap. 'Mrs. Greyson … I

was just wondering when the post comes … I'm expecting something.'

No answer came. Slim quietly opened the door and found Mrs. Greyson slumped in her armchair, snoring quietly. An empty tumbler stood on a coffee table; next to it stood a bottle of supermarket-brand port.

Slim instinctively reached for the bottle, then drew back, clenching his fist, forcing it into his jacket pocket to keep it out of trouble. His other hand had tightened over the door jamb.

It appeared that Mrs. Greyson enjoyed a drink too. Slim glanced at the clock on the mantel, an ornate steel lump with none of the finesse of the one he had found on the moor.

2.15 p.m.

He went out and quietly closed the door. If Mrs. Greyson wanted to get drunk in the middle of the afternoon, that was her business.

As he headed back out, this time to the bus stop, he wondered if he wasn't getting a little too caught up in Amos's Birch's disappearance. After all, it had happened more than twenty years ago. What could he possibly discover that the police investigation had missed?

He had been called reckless more than once during his ramshackle career as a private eye. He had stumbled into the profession through a lack of better options, and found he had a certain lateral way of thinking which gave him a knack for figuring out a situation. Yet, since quitting drinking he had lost a little of his edge, and the temptation to turn back to the bottle was becoming a garrulous voice in a quiet room.

16

PLYMOUTH WAS A BUSTLING HISTORICAL CITY STILL IN full swing when Slim got off the bus just after 5 p.m. He walked quickly through the shopping district and reached the town hall just half an hour before closing. A rather disgruntled clerk led him to the marriage registration department, where another clerk seemed just as frustrated at his late request.

'Tell me once again,' said the clerk, a stone-faced middle aged woman with a habit of tugging at the left horn of her old-fashioned spectacles, something which had over time left her glasses sitting slightly lopsided on the bridge of her nose.

'I'm trying to track down an old friend,' Slim said. 'I believe she might have married since I knew her.'

'What are the last details you have?'

'Celia Birch, of Worth Farm, Trelee, Bodmin, Cornwall.'

'Give me a minute. Take a seat, please.'

Slim flicked through a magazine on fly fishing for a while before the clerk called him back over.

'I'm sorry, sir, but I have nothing. No one by that name has registered a marriage in this district.'

'Okay, not to worry.'

'Sorry I couldn't help.'

'Thanks anyway.'

Slim headed out into the evening. Plymouth's shopping centre was shutting down for the night, and bars were beginning to open. Slim thrust his hands into his pockets and walked past the beckoning lights with his head down, feeling, for the first time in a while, a hollowness, a sense of absence, that there was an empty part of him that needed to be filled. Once, drink had done it, succeeding in drowning out a sense of failure that a succession of short-lived lovers had been unable to do. Now he found himself facing that beacon of disaster as his fingers slipped through the case of Amos Birch's disappearance.

He had grasped it because it gave him something where there was otherwise nothing, but now the void was opening, yawning in front of him, drawing him in.

At the end of the street, he stopped outside the door of the last pub. After a moment's hesitation, he pushed through the door and went inside.

17

'WHAT HAPPENED TO YOU, MR. HARDY?'

Slim rubbed his eyes. 'I think I got hit by a car.'

'Are you sure? Do need me to call someone?'

Slim shook his head, wincing at the ache in his neck. He remembered trying to walk through a punch as he might once have done during a brawl back in his army days, but it had proven as stupid an idea as it felt now with a hangover carving out the inside of his skull.

Only a doctor could say whether the punch had caused more damage than the tabletop that had arrested his fall, but now both eyes were bordered by an eerily symmetrical crescent of purple bruising, while the split lip caused by a second assailant seemed to exist solely to prevent him smiling at the absurdity of his situation.

'I'd also like to ask that if you're planning to stay out late then to please tell me in advance,' Mrs. Greyson added.

'I, um, just went out for an early walk,' Slim said. 'To clear my head.'

'Well, you left the door unlocked.'

'Ah, sorry.'

'Will you be having breakfast?'

'Is it possible I could take it up to my room? I'm not really feeling up to company.'

Even though he still appeared to be the guesthouse's only guest, Mrs. Greyson sighed. 'Normally I'd say no, but for you, Mr. Hardy, I'll make an exception. Just this once.'

He waited while she prepared a tray, memories of the evening before slowly coming back. What he had said or done to start the fight remained a mystery, and the lack of any scuffs or marks on his knuckles showed it had been one-sided. The park bench that had been last night's bed had left him with acute back stiffness, and he had somehow torn half of the sole from his left shoe.

An early morning Plymouth-to-Camelford bus had dropped him off on the A39 near the Penleven turning, and an hour's walk down winding lanes had sobered him up. The food had been cooked with less care than usual, but the coffee was a dark pool of clarity, so he thanked Mrs. Greyson and headed upstairs with his tray.

He wanted to crawl into his bed and die, but there was something he needed to check first. He had photographed all the articles he had read about Amos's disappearance, and now he scrolled through them, sure the information he required was there somewhere.

Merrifield.

Mary Birch's maiden name.

It was a casual way to avoid the public eye, but one not unexpected after your mother far outlived your father.

Slim lifted the phonebook he had borrowed from the table in the hall and there she was.

Merrifield, C., Parkwood Close, Tavistock, Devon.

She hadn't gone far at all, but when communities were so tightknit, twenty miles was the other side of the world.

Satisfied that the beating had rattled the thoughts around in his head enough to present a new lead, Slim downed the bitter, lukewarm coffee and climbed into bed.

18

'I'M PRETTY SURE I HAD NOTHING TO DO WITH THAT,' Michael said, leaning on a spade, his exposed arms slick with sweat despite the February cold. 'Although it crossed my mind the other night.'

'I had a meeting with a concrete slab,' Slim said. 'It wasn't pleased to see me.'

'I'm not pleased to see you either. What do you want?'

Slim gazed out across the field toward the bump of Rough Tor in the distance.

'This is going to sound pretty intrusive, but I want to ask you about Amos Birch.'

'Pretty intrusive? Who do you think you are?'

'I'm a private investigator, and I'm investigating the disappearance of Mr. Birch.' As soon as the words were out, Slim felt a surge of embarrassment at his attempt to sound authoritative. Michael, clearly not falling for the trick, shook his head.

'Private investigator, you say? So someone hired you, did they? Who might that be?'

'If you don't want to talk, that's fine. But if you have nothing to hide, it won't bother you, will it?'

Michael threw the spade aside and marched up to where Slim leaned on a field gate.

'Why don't you get lost?' he said.

Slim held his ground. 'Did you kill him, Michael?'

Michael balled his fists. 'You've got a nerve, asking me that.'

Slim remembered the eyes of young soldiers after they'd made a combat kill, the way they would glaze when spoken to, a part of their mind forevermore elsewhere, looking down the barrel of a gun at splash of colour behind a jerking head, or a tangle of rags lying in the street.

Michael's eyes shone with anger, but there was no guilt. Slim didn't want to consider being wrong, but he couldn't see murderer in Michael's eyes.

'Did you?'

'I had nothing to do with it.'

'What about Celia?'

'What about her?'

'Did you know her well? Do you think she had anything to do with her father's disappearance?'

Michael's face was a thundercloud. He glared at Slim with undisguised hatred, but there was something else there too: regret.

'You should stay out of people's business. We don't need your type round here, digging up the past.'

'What is there to dig up, Michael? The skeletal remains of an old man's body?'

Michael scowled. 'It's a figure of speech. If you don't mind, I have work to do.'

Slim returned to where his bike lay on the grass verge, leaving Michael to finish repairing a stone wall beside a stile. As he lifted his bike, he turned back quickly, just quick enough to catch Michael doing the same thing.

There had been no murder in Michael's eyes, but there had been enough knowing to ensure Slim would definitely be talking to him again.

19

After leaving Michael, Slim caught a bus to Tavistock and made his way to Parkwood Close. Celia's house was on a meandering terrace of Sixties-era houses. It lacked the architectural beauty of the older part of town but was pleasant enough, too narrow for much traffic and with a leafy park across the street.

Slim bought a newspaper in a corner shop then sat on a bench which had a view of Celia's front door through a screen of trees, idly scanning through pages of gossip and football reports as he waited for her to appear.

An hour later, having seen no one, he was almost done with the few interesting articles and had turned his attention to the growing tremble in his hands. He checked his watch. Half past five. It was almost late enough to be acceptable, so he gave in to his cravings and headed for the corner shop. A quart would be enough, perhaps, to keep him alert for a few more hours, and if he was careful, it might get him right through until bed.

He was halfway there, head down, hands in pockets and moving with a nervous desperation, when he almost bumped into a woman walking quickly the other way.

'Oh, sorry.'

The woman glanced up then stepped around him, turning her eyes down, increasing her pace.

Slim's heart jumped. Her age was about right. So was the kind of lingering but weathered attractiveness which might have once pulled men's strings. Before he could get control of his tongue, he blurted: 'Celia. Wait.'

She paused just long enough to tell him his hunch was right. She glanced back then shook her head, hurrying on. Slim remembered how he must look: gaunt, bruised, his clothes tattered and dirty.

'Celia … Ms. Birch—wait, please. I don't mean you any harm.'

She took a few steps, then stopped. She took a long breath as though a conversation with a stranger was a rare event, then slowly turned around, her eyes lifting. A bob of mousy brown hair was almost army-like in its accuracy, shadowing a square face which appeared lineless until she lifted her head enough for a nearby streetlight to catch it. Eyes that couldn't stay still flicked from the road to the terrace to back to Slim's.

'What do you want? How do you know my name?'

'Ms. Birch … I didn't mean to alarm you but … my name is Slim Hardy. This is going to sound stupid, but I'm a private investigator. I've been looking for your father.'

She frowned, cocking her head. 'Why?'

'Look, can we just talk?'

'No, I don't think so.' Celia turned and walked away.

'Ms. Birch—wait!'

'This is harassment,' she shouted back over her shoulder. 'Don't think I won't call the police.' To emphasise her point, she waved a mobile phone in the air as her heels clacked away along the pavement.

Slim hesitated. He had briefly seen the inside of one prison cell and had no intention of seeing the inside of another. Sometimes certain things went on when cameras were turned away. Forces personnel resented acts of violence between their own, and retaliated in their own particular style. Memories of the slap of the rubber hose on the back of his legs sometimes woke him at night, but this could be his only chance. If Celia ran, he might never find her again.

'Ms. Birch … I want to know what happened to your father, Amos.

Celia flapped a hand over her shoulder. 'He abandoned us, that's all. Happens every day, doesn't it?'

Slim hurried to keep up as she increased her pace again.

'And I also want to know about Charlotte.'

Celia stopped dead, Slim almost bumping into her. The bag she carried fell from one hand, her phone from the other.

In the distance a siren began to wail. Celia stood, hands dropping to her sides, looking up at the sky. Then, as she turned, Slim realised the sound was no siren.

With gritted teeth, Celia kicked off her heels, scooped one up then ran at him, the shoe held up like a club.

'Celia—' Slim started, but it was too late. The hard flat square at the end of Celia's heel swung toward his face.

20

'I'M EX-ARMY,' SLIM SAID, HANDING BACK CELIA'S shoe as she sat up on the grass and wiped dirt off her blouse. 'It's been nearly twenty years, but they drilled us pretty well. Muscle memory. If you'd tried that with a gun, I'd have broken your arm.'

'Do you want me to say thanks?'

Slim fell quiet. He looked at a clump of fresh daffodil leaves—the flowers still a few days off—as they swayed in the evening breeze.

'I don't know what I want,' he said. 'I don't know why I'm here really, if I'm honest about it.'

'Then why are you?'

Slim frowned. 'It's an addiction, isn't it? It's no different to the booze. Once I start, I can't stop. I have to see it out, for better or … worse.'

'And my father is your pet project? Your little holiday mystery? Honestly, most people just go to the beach.'

'I tan badly. Rain and cold suit me better.'

For the first time, the hint of a smile appeared on Celia's lips.

'Yeah, me too.' She sighed as she put her shoes back on. 'So you're ex-army? Why'd you quit?'

'I didn't quit. I got thrown out. "Dishonourable discharge" was their pretty little label. I tried to kill someone.'

'Isn't that the whole point?'

Slim shrugged. 'It depends on the circumstances. On this occasion, no. I jumped through their hoops, did my time, and ended up at the back of another unemployment queue. When you like a drink it's not easy to hold down a job, however, so I figured I'd use some of what I learned in the Armed Forces for private investigation.'

'You're not being very private about it.'

Slim grimaced. 'On my last case I had a few problems, both with the people involved and the police. This is supposed to be a recuperation holiday, but I can't just sit around and watch TV, or walk on the moor. I'm not that kind of guy. After a while it all starts to look the same.'

'My father would have bit your head off for saying that about the moors. He loved living on the edge of that muddy shithole.'

'Your father, right. When I heard about his disappearance it got me intrigued. I'm afraid I asked a few questions, many of which weren't welcome. But I figured that since I'd already upset most of the residents of Penleven, so I might as well go for the jackpot and see if I could upset you too.'

'Well, you've pulled it off.'

A hundred questions burned on Slim's tongue, but he remembered something told to him by an old friend from the Armed Forces who had worked as an interrogator during the Gulf War: sometimes silence is your greatest weapon. Questions are like missiles; they send people diving for cover. Stay quiet, give them time, and often your target will come out into the open.

'So, what is so interesting about my father?' she said at last, and Slim allowed himself an inward smile.

'Everything. People don't just disappear. They always go somewhere. They fall down a hole and die, or they run off and change their identity.'

'Whatever he did, he did a good job of it. You really want to know what happened? He walked off into the night and never came back. We had no idea it was coming, none whatsoever. The police combed every inch of that moor but they found no trace of him. Some footprints, that's all, but they lost his trail a few hundred metres from our house. Once you're away from the stream there's no mud, just that goddamn springy grass for miles and miles.'

'So who is Charlotte? What is so incendiary about the name that caused you to attack me?'

Celia's face turned dark. 'How did you hear that name?'

'Like I say, I got in a lot of people's faces.'

'You're lying.'

'Am I?'

Celia glared at him then looked away. 'Charlotte was my daughter.'

'Was?'

Celia lifted her head and stared at Slim with teary eyes. 'Are you sure you want to open this box? You won't like what you find.'

'It's too late.'

Celia shook her head. 'It's never too late. You should walk away while you have the chance. This haunts me, Slim. It doesn't need to haunt you, too.'

21

Much to Slim's disappointment, Celia, who claimed to be a nurse, had only been heading home to prepare for a night shift. In the face of his own refusal to expand on where he had heard Charlotte's name, she refused to give Slim any further details. She did, however, agree to meet him the following weekend.

To keep himself out of the nearest pub, he caught the evening bus back to Penleven, getting off in the dark at the stop half a mile out of the village.

Mrs. Greyson was waiting in the hall when he entered, but rather than berate him for his lateness as was usual, she held out a small package.

'I do apologise … this arrived for you yesterday. I'm not used to getting post for guests. I'm afraid I opened it by mistake.'

She didn't meet his eyes as he took it, but as soon as it was out of her hands she turned and retreated into the kitchen, busying herself with some washing up.

The package was from Kay. Slim took it up to his room, closing the door behind him. Enclosed was a color photocopy of the note, together with a typed letter from Kay explaining his thoughts its contents.

As he turned it over, Slim noticed a crease on one side. It had nothing to do with the way the letter was folded, but was more of a depression in the surface. Frowning, he held the letter under the corner lamp, holding it close to the light and tilting it until the creases showed as faint shadows.

Fingermarks creased the paper a third of the way up on each side. Mrs. Greyson, clearly not adept at subterfuge, had read it carefully before putting it away.

Slim read the note again then returned it to the envelope. Perhaps Mrs. Greyson had understood the message's cryptic meaning. It might have brought on her sudden drinking binge.

The TV was on in the living room when Slim reached the bottom of the stairs. He ran through varieties of the coming conversation in his mind, then took a deep breath and rapped lightly on the door.

When he received no answer, he opened it a crack, wondering if Mrs. Greyson had undertaken a repeat of the previous day and got sloshed in her armchair.

The living room, however, was empty.

Feeling like a night prowler, Slim crept through the room and peered into a private dining area that linked up with the kitchen accessible from the guest's dining room.

No sign of Mrs. Greyson. A half-finished cup of tea sat on the counter, and a home-life magazine lay open nearby, as though she had got up and left halfway through an article.

Slim retreated to the hall. He was turning to head back upstairs when the door bumped, startling him.

The latch was off, the loose fitting bolt left to be troubled by the wind.

Mrs. Greyson's boots were missing, but her handbag hung where it always did, on the umbrella stand inside the door.

If she had chosen to go out it was no business of Slim's, but as he headed up the stairs he couldn't help but find it unusual.

In the near month he had been staying at the guesthouse, he had never known Mrs. Greyson to go out at night.

Not ever.

22

'DID YOU SLEEP WELL, MR. HARDY?'

Slim forced a smile. At least his beat up face would hide that he'd stayed up late waiting for Mrs. Greyson to return. He had fallen asleep just after two, but if she'd come back earlier she'd been quiet about it. Despite the presumed lack of sleep, she was no more irascible than usual.

'There was something of a storm last night, I believe,' he said, hoping to coax a confession out of her. 'The wind was rattling the window. It kept me awake.'

She shook from the waist up, like a bird preening its feathers. 'I'll have someone come around promptly to fix it,' she said.

'It's not a problem—' Slim began, but Mrs. Greyson put up a hand to indicate the matter was closed.

'Will you be going out today, Mr. Hardy?'

Slim smiled. 'I thought I might take a walk on the moor.'

'There's rain forecast,' Mrs. Greyson said.

'Isn't there always? I'll be careful.'

Outside, he attempted to coax his limited detection skills into finding whatever trail she might have left, but aside from a single boot print in a patch of mud pooling in a hollow alongside the front step, there was nothing, and he quickly gave up. There was probably a simple explanation. He remembered her mentioning a bridge club, so perhaps she got together with all the other local gossips every month or so to review what news had come out of the village.

The rain Mrs. Greyson had predicted was pattering like fingers drumming on a windowsill by the time Slim reached the bus stop. When he alighted in Liskeard a couple of hours later, it had reverted to a more agreeable mist, just enough to keep his clothes sodden and his morale low, but not enough to make Slim miss the umbrella he hadn't brought.

Liskeard Comprehensive Secondary School was easy to find, and the fake BBC3 Staff card hanging around his neck felt as familiar as the last time he'd used it to get information. He waited until lines of small heads through windows told him class was in session then headed for the main entrance.

Schools had changed since his school days, he discovered. A lock and buzzer on the gate meant he had to state his purpose into a microphone and hold up his ID before being buzzed inside.

A receptionist was waiting for him. 'Mr. Lewis?'

'Call me Dan,' Slim said, giving his fake ID a nonchalant tap.

'You wanted to talk to someone concerning a Mr. Amos Birch?' she said, looking up from a handwritten note.

'Yes … I apologise for the abruptness of my visit. I came here on something of a whim. I very much doubt anyone can help me anyway, so I truly appreciate a few minutes of your time.'

'Not at all, not at all. So, you're from the BBC?'

'I'm a preliminary documentary researcher with BBC3,' Slim said, hoping an overload of jargon would slip through her defenses. 'I'm exploring the possibility of a film based on the disappearance of Amos Birch, the famous local clockmaker who lived over on Bodmin Moor. He attended this school. You're aware of that, I assume?'

'Well, yes, I do believe—'

'Note that I'm not researching an actual green-lighted film, but putting out feelers to see if there is enough material to invest in a potential project.'

'Excuse me while I make a quick inquiry.'

The receptionist leaned into a phone. Slim tried not to listen in, instead focusing his attention on the photographs framed on the walls around the reception desk. A couple of long-ago sports teams, an aerial shot of the school, a line of grey suits headlined by a *Staff of 2018* label. A couple of younger faces wore smiles: unbroken yet by the high seas of teaching; but most wore grim, hardened expressions like soldiers in the midst of a long campaign.

The receptionist put down the phone and looked up.

'The headmaster is out on business today, but our deputy head, Mr. Clair, will give you a few minutes.'

'Thanks.'

She led Slim to a plain office where a squat, balding man with a close resemblance to a toad sat behind a desk. Chubby fingers made a steeple amid greasy finger marks on the glossy Formica surface.

Slim introduced himself as Dan Lewis from BBC3, then let his mouth run for a few minutes with a half-cooked background story until finally Mr. Clair lifted a hand.

'So you'd like to know about Mr. Birch's school days, is that right?' the deputy head said, sounding only mildly more interested than he might hearing about a playground scuffle.

'I'm looking for old class photos, report cards, anything related to Amos Birch. My boss thinks his disappearance would make a good story, but we don't have much to go on, I'll admit.'

'Records going back that far will have been archived,' Mr. Clair said, his voice uncomfortably lilting for a man with such an intrusive presence. 'I can have someone dig them out, but I doubt they'd reveal much about the man.'

'That's not all I'm after,' Slim said. 'To make a documentary compelling, it needs a deeper aspect of storytelling. It needs a sensationalist angle.'

'I thought you came from the BBC, not *The Sun*.'

Slim wagged a theatrical finger, one slightly bent from a time long ago when an army-issued boot had fallen on it in anger.

'Ah, but the principle is the same. Amos Birch is one of this school's most prestigious former pupils. It's inconceivable that there wouldn't be tall tales about him.'

'Oh, I'm sure there are,' Mr. Clair said, fixing Slim with a cold stare. 'You're talking about a man who's been missing twenty-odd years, and was in his fifties then. It would have been way back in the Sixties when he attended this school, so there won't be anyone on the staff who taught him.'

'You must know something about him, though.'

Mr. Clair shrugged. 'Some. I've heard the name a few times. I'm not a native of these parts though, so I never met the man. I knew him by reputation only.'

'It seems a lot of people did,' Slim said. 'But that's all they knew. I've found little except rumours.'

'Maybe that's all there are.' Mr. Clair abruptly stood up, the chair creaking its relief, but the desk shuddering as a monstrous body collided with it. 'I'll ask one of the office staff to take a look through the archives. If you leave a phone number, I'll have someone contact you if we find anything.'

Slim told Mr. Clair it was easier if he got back in touch after a week or so. The deputy head looked distrusting of Slim's explanation that he was staying somewhere with a poor signal, even if it was the only part of his charade that was true.

He left, uncertain whether he'd gained anything other than a few more suspicious glances. He wondered whether he had enough new information to justify a coffee stop, or even an hour in the pub. The school had proved a dead end, but there was a chance something might reveal itself in the archives, even if it was just the name of a retired teacher who might remember Amos as a boy.

It was still early. Beer would be calming, but coffee more productive. Slim remembered a little place not far from the bus station, but he was only halfway across the school's front car park to the main road when someone hailed him from behind.

A boyish-faced man of about Slim's age was walking briskly toward him, while simultaneously trying to tuck in a section of shirt which had come loose during his pursuit. The man had an eagerness Slim understood, his eyes hungrily eyeing a few minutes of TV fame.

'Nick Jones,' the man said, holding out a hand whose palm had the clammy softness of someone who considered manual labour to be straightening a shelf of books. 'I'm the Year Eight form teacher?'

Slim nodded, unsure whether this was information he was supposed to know. He waited for the man to continue.

'You're from the BBC, right? Brenda mentioned in the staffroom there was someone from the TV here.'

Slim hid a smile. 'That's right.'

'Look, I shouldn't really be saying this, but I might have some info I can throw your way if you have time for a short conv?'

The man's habit of speaking like an email message was grating Slim's senses, but he feigned an enthusiastic nod and pulled a notebook from his pocket.

'What can you tell me, Nick?'

'I met Amos Birch a couple of times. That's who you're asking about, right? Back when I was just starting out.' He grinned. 'I'm older than I look.'

Slim resisted an urge to punch him. 'Go on.'

'I was Celia Birch's form teacher during her GCSE year. You know, his daughter? Amos came down with his wife for parents' evenings.'

Slim sensed a lead, but at the ring of a bell in the background, Nick Jones glanced over his shoulder, then whistled through his teeth and looked back at Slim with frustration etched on his face.

'Are you okay to talk now?' Slim asked.

'Playground monitor duty, I'm afraid.'

'Tonight?'

'PTA meeting.' Nick Jones whistled again. 'The duties never end.'

Slim looked at the calendar in the front of his notebook. 'How about Sunday?'

Nick Jones nodded. 'Sure. Here's my number. You know, there was always something wrong about that family,' he said. 'More than just not right, but fully wrong. You got me?'

'Give me an example.'

'Like Celia. Good girl, a little sharp-tongued but she handed her work in, looked set for decent GCSEs, then she stops showing up. She's gone, quit.'

'Why?'

'She turned sixteen. She was allowed to leave. She gave that as her reason on her leavers' form, so I was told.'

'But?'

Nick Jones made a show of a grimace. Slim watched him, waiting for the inevitable confession.

'Generally only the clowns and the wasters drop out, the ones who are losing valuable shelf-stacking income by staying for their exams. Celia wasn't one of those kids. She was bright. But the kids used to talk, didn't they? Said the worst things.'

'Tell me the absolute worst.'

Nick Jones stuffed his hands into his trouser pockets even though it wasn't so cold, then theatrically puffed out his cheeks.

'They say she got knocked up. And he was the father.'

'Who?'

Nick glanced back, as though expecting a crowd of teachers had appeared from nowhere to listen in on his revelation. When he turned back, his voice was low, conspiratorial:

'Amos. Her dad.'

23

CELIA WAS SITTING ON A ROCK, FACING SOUTH ACROSS the moor toward Jamaica Inn, nestled in a cleft in the hill, its peace disturbed by the roar of traffic on the A38 to Bodmin. As Slim came up behind her, she lifted a flask to her lips and took a long swallow of a liquid which steamed around her face.

'Do you think we'll be overheard?' Slim said, throwing down his pack as he sat beside her, rubbing a spot on his thigh where he had failed to see an outcropping rock. 'I saw a couple of suspicious-looking sheep during the hike up. I'm pretty sure one was wearing a wire.'

Celia smiled. Dressed in hiking gear that was either new or rarely used, she looked far different to the bitter-faced woman Slim had met on the Tavistock street. She had tied up her hair, and the attractiveness that had been a mere residue now showed through. She was older, wiser, wearier, but the face of a woman once capable of luring men from their wives was apparent in the soft lines of her face.

'I wanted to make sure you were really keen. I've buried all this. I'm not digging it up for some timewaster. Drink?' She held out the flask.

'What is it?'

'Mulled wine.'

Slim snatched it out of her hands, took a swig, then scowled. 'It's tea.'

'How good's your imagination?'

'It gets better the more I drink.'

Celia nodded as she looked out across the moor. Slim glanced at her, then followed her gaze over the rocky hillside, the distant stands of trees, a small lake, the rocky banks of a moorland stream. Neither spoke for a long time.

'It's pretty, I suppose,' Slim said at last. 'I prefer the city, but it's far too easy to wreck yourself. At least out here you can get some fresh air.'

'There's not enough of you out here,' Celia said, rather cryptically. 'In the city people are too busy to care, but in the country we're all just frameworks for other people to fill in the gaps. We're all just a story constantly being rewritten and overwritten to a point where we're no longer sure who we are.'

'And who are you?' Slim asked.

'I'm not sure. All the things I was, I'm no longer. I was a daughter, and I was a mother, and I was almost a wife. Now I suppose I'm just me. Celia.'

'It could be worse,' Slim said. 'You could be a pair

of boots sitting on the sand, everything you were vanished in an instant.'

'Empty boots?'

Slim shivered as he shook his head. 'They're not empty.'

Celia was quiet a moment. Then she said: 'Tell me how you heard the name Charlotte. Don't lie to me. I'll know if you do. Only three people knew my daughter's name. I buried one. The other I lost. And the third is me.'

'I found something buried near the summit of Rough Tor, wrapped in a plastic bag. You know how the cliché goes? I literally tripped over it, almost broke my damn ankle. It was an old, damaged clock, and in the back of it I found a note. The paper was water-damaged, so I had a friend who works in translation and forensic linguistics open it. I brought with me what he found. Here.'

He handed Celia a plastic file taken from his rucksack. He watched her as she opened it and looked the sheets over one by one. Her hands visibly shook as she leaned closer. At one point a printed photograph slipped through her fingers, and only a quick dive by Slim prevented a gust of wind from taking it away downslope.

'And those are photos of the clock I found the note inside,' he said, handing it back to her. 'I have all the originals stashed at the guesthouse.'

'I'd like to see it.' She lifted a hand to her cheek and flicked away a tear before it had much chance to leave a trail. 'My god. This is crazy.'

Slim waited. He wanted to ask, but Celia was staring at the copy of the note, her lower lip trembling.

At last she looked up. 'Who are you, Mr. Hardy?'

'Call me Slim. Everyone does.'

'Slim. Who are you really?'

'I'm a private investigator.'

'No. That's just a label. Who is the man behind it?'

Slim felt uncomfortable beneath her searching gaze, but the sorrow in her eyes suggested a woman searching for kinship.

'I used to be a husband. I was a brave and powerful man and I worked as a soldier. Then I found ghosts waiting for me beside an Iraqi highway. Real ones, not the kind in stories, and they wouldn't let me go. I never recovered, although I played the game a few more years. When I was about done with war and ready to come home, I lost my wife to a butcher called Mr. Stiles, my unborn child to a packet of prescription pills, and my sanity to a sideways glance and a razor blade. That's what I was. What am I now? I'm not sure. I'm an alcoholic. I'm also a lost boy, searching for meaning and purpose in life. With each case I pray that I'll find it, and while I haven't yet, I'm not done trying.'

'Perhaps you'll find it in the pot of gold at the end of the Birch family rainbow.'

'Maybe.'

'I had a daughter,' Celia said, playing with the skin on the back of her hands. 'She was three years old. Her name was Charlotte. And I had a father. Amos. They were the two dearest people in the world to me, and one day they disappeared. I wasn't a great mother. I tried my best but I was too young, and to be honest, my own mother was hardly a good role model. When I failed my father picked up the slack. He was always with Charlotte, to the point where it made me jealous to see them together. Then one night, he carried her off onto the moor and he never came back.'

Slim let out a long breath. 'He took your daughter with him?'

'Yes. They disappeared together.'

'But how? I read nothing about him being with a little girl.'

'No one knew she existed. She was three when she vanished. I wanted to call the police but my mother … she….'

Slim put a hand on her arm. 'It's okay—'

Celia jerked her arm away. 'No, it's not okay. It was never okay. I was young and stupid and I let that woman manipulate me with her lies.'

'What woman?'

'My mother, Mary.' Celia bared her teeth in a way that stripped away her humanity and make her into something wild and feral.

'Oh, I'm sure you've heard all sorts of lies about my family, but there was only ever one true monster. My mother, Mary Birch. If there was a worse woman in the world, I've never met her.'

24

'SHE TOLD ME I'D GO TO PRISON IF I WENT TO THE police,' Celia said. 'She managed to convince me I'd be in serious trouble for never registering Charlotte, even though it was her decision to keep Charlotte's existence a secret. Everything was her idea. My father … he was eccentric. Maybe a little autistic even, but he was never officially diagnosed. He could make the most beautiful, ornate clocks, but in other senses he was helpless. He couldn't cook. My mother used to tell him what to wear each morning. Everything, all his international acclaim, it was down to my mother and her obsession with getting him up on a pedestal.'

'She sounds terrifying.'

'After they disappeared, she convinced me to say nothing about Charlotte, told me she'd frame me, ensure I was implicated in both my father's disappearance and that of Charlotte's, because it had to be my fault, didn't it? My daughter whom no one knew about, she was the catalyst for his disappearance, and who did she belong to? Me. I couldn't escape it. My mother drummed it into me at every available opportunity, and eventually I stopped fighting it and just believed her. Over time life just became a habit, and then she was slipping so close to her grave that I just waited her out. I got rid of the farm as soon as I could.'

'I don't know what to say. I doubt "I'm sorry" would quite cover it.'

Celia smiled. 'You don't need to say anything. It's helped a lot to finally tell someone. Catharsis, of a sort. My father was a good man. At the time I blamed him, because I felt he should have stood up to her so much more. My mother set the rules and pulled the strings, and my father let her. Charlotte … I don't know what went through his mind when he took her, but perhaps he wanted to take her away from the hostility of that place. Most people thought he died somewhere out on the moor, but they didn't know about Charlotte. My father, he could have set up a life somewhere else, but she would have been noticed. He might have just left her on the steps of an orphanage, put her in care. I don't know. She could still be alive.'

'But, couldn't she tell them—'

Celia lifted a hand. 'Charlotte couldn't speak. She was mute. Perhaps she was just a late developer … I'll never know. But at the time I lost her, she'd never uttered a single word.'

Slim put out an arm as Celia leaned in to his shoulder, the tears coming fast. He looked out at the beautiful, rugged view and wondered how it must feel to see ghosts out there, shadows moving among the scattered field of stones that could be a daughter or a father returning home.

'There's more,' Celia said, 'but I can't face it right now. I have a place I need to be tonight, but we can meet again soon. I doubt you'll be able to help me find either of them … but you might.'

'I wasn't looking for a job,' Slim said.

Celia smiled, then gave him the kind of affectionate pat on the cheek a mother might give to a grown son.

'Well, you've found one.'

25

'I had a call about a booking,' Mrs. Greyson said. 'A party of six. I'd need all three rooms available.'

Slim decided to call her bluff. 'I was planning to stay at least another week. The story of Amos Birch hasn't run its course for me just yet. It's quite intriguing. I'm interested in investigating it further.'

Mrs. Greyson rolled her eyes. 'All you'll find there is an endless series of lies and rumours. You should give it up. Everyone else did.'

'You know, everyone talks about Amos Birch, but what of his wife? What of Mary? No one has much to say about her.'

Mrs. Greyson visibly recoiled. 'There's not much to say. She was a hard-faced old farm wife. That's all really.'

'I was just thinking that it's possible she killed him.'

The cup Mrs. Greyson held struck the floor with a crack like a gun going off. Slim scrambled to pick up pieces of crockery as Mrs. Greyson stood wringing her hands as though to punish them for a misgiving.

'Let me help you with that—'

Mrs. Greyson brushed him out of the way with a full flourish of her arm. 'I'll deal with it, Mr. Hardy. Honestly, if I had other guests I'd be inclined to ask you to leave.'

'Didn't you say something about a party of six?'

'It was just an enquiry,' she snapped, then retreated into the kitchen before returning with a dustpan and brush. 'You should be careful about saying such things,' she continued, sweeping up chips of china clay. 'Some people might be a little sensitive.'

'It wasn't meant as an accusation, just a possibility.'

'It was impossible that she could have killed him,' Mrs. Greyson said. 'Mary Birch was in a wheelchair. She had some sort of degenerative disease. The only weapon she had was her mouth, and while that was bad enough, it couldn't have caused a murder.'

'Oh. I didn't know.'

'She was a thorny old woman,' Mrs. Greyson added, 'but she would never have hurt Amos even if she could have. He was everything to her.'

'As her husband, you'd hope he'd be.'

'I didn't mean it like that,' Mrs. Greyson said with a sudden venom surprising even for her. 'She was a no one. Amos was her ticket to a better life. She was fiercely protective of him. You couldn't get near him unless she said so. She ruled that accursed place.'

Slim nodded. 'Their marriage must have been tense.'

Mrs. Greyson gave a dismissive shrug. 'I wouldn't know, would I? Not my place to go putting my nose into other people's business.'

And with that, she disappeared back into the kitchen. By the time Slim had finished his breakfast, she still hadn't come back out.

26

Nick Jones kept looking over his shoulder into the scraggly stands of moorland trees that lined Siblyback Reservoir, as though searching for a hidden camera crew. He had even dressed for the occasion: his hair recently trimmed, a tweed jacket turned up at the collar as though he expected Michael Caine to pull up in a Bentley and whisk him off to a covert operation on the continent.

'Were you worried we would be overheard?' Slim asked as the wind buffeted off the water's surface like a landing biplane and curled its chilly fingers down his neck. He wished he'd worn a thicker sweater under his light wind-cheater, but he hadn't been expecting a drive out of Liskeard up to the lake.

'In small towns, everyone knows everyone else,' Nick said. 'It's best to be safe. Plus, I like it up here. It's peaceful, but rugged in its way.'

Slim considered suggesting Nick looked into a career

as an actor. He was already convinced he was wasting his time, when Nick added, 'You know, there was always something wrong about that family.'

Slim stuffed his hands into his pockets as far as they would go and asked, 'How was Celia at school? Generally? Good girl? Withdrawn?'

Nick smiled, nodding at the same time as though flicking through a picture book of memories. 'She was a talker. One of those kids always leaning over the desk behind, laughing and joking. She was fairly spiky; kept it just the safe side of rude.'

'She liked to talk back at the teacher?'

'Yeah, if she thought she could get away with it.'

'Did she bully other kids?'

'Not that I recall. Certainly she had a lot to say, but her attention was always wandering. She couldn't focus on anyone long enough to bully them. She certainly wasn't bullied, though. No one would dare.'

'She was tough?'

'Oh, yeah. But her mother was a battleaxe. You could see where it came from. I'd have her in there on parents' evening and she'd snap at Celia right in front of me. Her dad would sit there quietly, watching everything. Celia would redden, then glare at her father as though wanting his defense. It never came.'

'He didn't stick up for her?'

'He was a bit creepy, was Amos Birch. He'd be gazing off into space then he'd turn and look at you, but it wouldn't be just a look, it would be a stare, and he wouldn't blink, just keep staring until you looked away. Then you'd look back and he'd still be staring, only to give a little shake of his head as though he'd fallen asleep while looking at you, with his eyes open.'

'I've heard he was a little autistic.'

'Maybe. He was odd for sure. And you never know with quiet types, do you?'

'Celia … did she ever have boyfriends?'

Nick laughed. 'She was one of those girls forever making up or breaking up. I'm sure you remember the type. Fun to be around if you were part of the in-crowd.'

Slim nodded. 'Avoided a couple of them myself.'

'You must have been a hit, seeing as you ended up working for the BBC.'

Slim almost forgot himself before he remembered the guise he was operating under.

'Well, you know, it's just a job, and at fourteen I was still a kid like everyone else.'

'I'd love to be involved with television,' Nick said.

Involved. Not "on", or "work in", but involved. Slim suppressed a sigh.

'Nick, what can you tell me about Celia leaving school?'

'Rumours were everywhere before she dropped out,' Nick said. 'You could sense something was up in her demeanor. I mean, she was so full of herself. Then, like overnight, she turned all withdrawn, like someone had finally pulled her down a peg or two.'

Slim frowned. 'Could it have been trouble at home?'

Nick laughed. 'She was fifteen. I doubt a day passed when there wasn't trouble at home. Anyway, it looked as though the little slapper got taught a lesson.'

'Little slapper?'

Nick shrugged, giving Slim a guilty smile. 'A bad choice of words, I guess. But kind of appropriate. Used to flirt with me something rotten. I was only in my early twenties at the time, so wasn't much older than the kids, really. She was a pretty girl, was Celia. Boys were always after her, and she was always out at those discos they'd let the kids into. The ones where they all start getting together. Don't need to think too hard about what went on, do you?'

Slim shrugged, a little concerned about Nick's slut-shaming of a former pupil, but then he wouldn't be the first teacher to fancy one of his class. There were stories in the news all the time about the ones who had taken it too far.

Nick was still talking. 'This was back in the nineties when girls would be going out with t-shirts with "whore" and "easy" and that kind of thing written on them. Love, if you could call it that, was as easy to come by as it was in the sixties.'

'And Celia was one of those girls?'

'Walking down the corridor on a Monday morning, you'd overhear all kinds. That girl was always with someone, if the rumour mill was true.'

Slim nodded. 'And you said she dropped out?'

Nick shifted, tossing his hair in the wind. 'You want to get this stuff down on tape?'

Slim shook his head then remembered what organisation Nick thought he worked for. 'Not yet,' he said with a smile. 'But this is good stuff. This is exactly what we're looking for. Tell me about what you told me before.'

Nick, clearly in love with his own voice, nodded. 'She started putting on weight. Like, suddenly. You remember how except for those girls with the thyroid, all they cared about was keeping thin enough to get hooked up on a weekend? Well, a couple of girls called her out on her weight gain in games class, so I heard. Then, we're a month from the GCSEs, and she's gone, dropped out.'

'She was sixteen, though, right? You can leave school at sixteen.'

'Not many do, not these days. She got good grades, she'd have done okay. Not straight As, but she'd have passed everything without much fuss.'

'And you told me that rumour about her father? If she was as promiscuous as you've suggested, couldn't it have been anyone?'

'See, that's where it got odd. School rumours are all over the place. They change with the Cornish weather. But for this, they polarized. Everyone was saying the same thing.'

'And what makes you think it wasn't just a hot rumour that got jumped on? Kids can be worse pack animals than wild dogs.'

Nick gave a frantic shake of his head. 'See, you'd need to understand the Birch family dynamic. The mother, she was a dragon. Celia hated her. The dad, Amos, he was quiet, introverted, but nice. Pure, even, in a simplistic kind of way. Celia despised her mother, and I mean *despised*. You could see her doing something just to hurt Mary. But you know what made it so much more concrete?'

'What?'

'Kids were saying it came from Celia herself. That she said her own dad got her knocked up.'

27

AFTER NICK HAD LEFT, LEAVING SLIM A HANDWRITTEN note with his phone number and a couple of email addresses, Slim found a printing shop on the high street to print out the photos he had taken of the farmyard at Worth Farm. With the ones he had taken of Amos Birch's old workshop, he first enlarged them until the door and its padlock filled the screen, so that if such things had brand markings, an expert in the field would know.

Using the shop's fax, he sent them to a London number then went outside to make a call.

'Alan, it's Slim,' he said, when the voice of an old friend came on the line. 'I need a favour.'

Alan Coaker, an old roommate during their training days at Harrogate, coughed a punctured laugh. The gravelly sound of his voice suggested he was yet to quit the twenty-a-day habit he'd maintained throughout their time together in the army.

'John? Is that you? Going by Slim now, are you?'

'It's been a while.'

'Been a while since you've called me, too. Wasn't that last time when you wanted to break into your girlfriend's house?'

'Ex-wife. Although we weren't ex at the time, and it was still my house.'

'That was it. What happened? You just get let out?'

'I got drunk instead.'

'Figures. Always had more bark than bite, didn't you, John? Anyway, while I'd love to chat, I have customers waiting. What do you want?'

'I've just sent you a fax.'

'Don't you do emails yet? I guess I'd better go turn the old thing on, then. It's in a box in the back room somewhere.'

Alan put down the phone. Slim, unsure whether Alan was joking, waited while his old squad mate was gone. It sounded as though Alan was doing well for himself. They had served together in the first Gulf War, but unlike Slim, Alan had got out with his record intact after two decades of unblemished service, and had used his generous payoff to start up a locksmith's company in London.

'Got it, Slim. What is it? These pictures something I need to shred after I finish this call?'

'I hope not. I need to get into that shed. I need to know what that lock is and how I can get past it.'

'Isn't there a window?'

'Barred.'

'And I'm guessing the owners don't want you poking about?'

'Correct.'

'So what you're after is some kind of device to get you through that bolt and chain?'

'That's right.'

There was a pause. Then Alan said, 'I can courier you something if you've got money to pay and an address. Tomorrow morning. That work?'

'Yeah. Thanks.'

'No problem.'

Slim hung up, feeling satisfied. The shed might hold nothing of interest, but it was a lead until Slim's curiosity was satisfied.

Liskeard was a pretty uninspiring place compared to some of the Cornish towns Slim had visited. With a couple of hours to kill before the bus back to Camelford —from where he had another depressing wait for the Bodmin Moor Loop Line bus—he headed for the town library. There, he logged on to a computer to do a little background research before his next meeting with Celia.

An old missing persons' archive had nothing new on Amos Birch. Celia had mentioned a police investigation, so unless Amos had been declared legally dead, he ought to still be listed. Celia's attitude suggested Slim was looking for a body, but the archive raised a question he would need her to clarify.

Neither was there a listing for Charlotte Birch. The poor little girl had come into the world and left it without leaving a single mark of her being.

Next, he attempted a search for unidentified bodies,

but there was no publicly searchable database. He had a fanciful idea that Amos could be wandering around somewhere with no memory, while the only articles he found about famous amnesiacs were for people whose identity had eventually been traced.

As he retreated to a coffee shop to lick his wounds, he began to feel like a rat trapped in a corner. He needed a break or the wheels would come off his fledgling investigation.

There was Celia, of course, who had the most information. But if a police investigation had failed to find anything, what chance did he have?

Of course, he had the one clue they didn't: the unearthed clock.

He had brought the papers Kay had sent him, and now he spread them out on the table, looking for something he had missed.

There was the message: *Charlotte, your time is forever. I will wait for you, always,* and the illegible second line which could have been a continuation. Then there was the initial A, which could possibly be an M.

Slim had sent some photographs to Kay and received Kay's notes in return. The carved animals shared a connection in that they were all British wildlife: deer, foxes, badgers, owls, otters, rabbits. Now that Slim looked at it again, they all crowded around the clock face, looking up at the little door as though waiting for the cuckoo to appear. The door itself was a slightly darker brown to the rest of the clock, as though made of a different kind of wood. Slim had naturally assumed the wood had been bought from a DIY store of some kind, but now he wondered if it might not have a greater significance. It was the kind of thing a police investigation might assign a team to, but it could also be a long and arduous dead end.

Celia remained his key witness. There had to be something she knew which would prove a vital clue.

He glanced at a clock above the baristas' counter: five thirty. Celia, who had said she worked in Plymouth, was due off work at six, and she had offered to pick him up and drive him back to the guesthouse, giving him some more information during the round trip journey back through Liskeard to her home in Tavistock.

It was a short walk up to the town hall where she had asked him to wait. A light drizzle made everything damp and it was already fully dark.

The car that pulled up was a battered Rover Metro. He had expected something better of a woman who claimed to be a nurse, but as someone who had totaled his last car he could understand why a person possessing a reckless streak would go for something easily replaced without sentiment. In its tight interior they were closer than Slim felt comfortable, meaning he had to press against the door to avoid leaning against Celia's arm. In the gloom cast by the dashboard lights she was patches of skin and occasional glitters of eyes. She smelled of cigarettes and flapped a hand as Slim plugged in his belt, as though to apologise.

'I'm trying to quit,' she said.

'Trying's a good place to start,' Slim said. 'I do a lot of it.'

She pulled out into Liskeard's late commuter traffic. 'Have you picked up any leads yet?'

'My best one just picked me up.'

'I was afraid you would say that.'

'I need you to tell me everything you can remember,' Slim said. 'Not just about the disappearances of your father and daughter, but other stuff too. Background stuff. Clues can hide in the most innocuous of places.'

'Where would you like me to start?'

'Your family. What other relations do you have? Anyone close?'

'I was an only child. My father was too, I believe. I had an aunt on my mother's side, but she died a few years before my father's disappearance. She lived in Reading. I only met her once; I don't think she got along with my mother.' She chuckled. 'Few people did.'

'You know, in the vast majority of murder cases, the killer is a relative or someone known to the family.'

'I've heard that too.'

'Who was Charlotte's father?'

The car jerked across the road, cutting into the path of an oncoming car before Celia got the vehicle under control. Slim let out a breath as the car passed harmlessly by, its horn blaring to remind them of how close they had come to a collision.

'Celia?'

Her hands had tightened on the wheel. 'Can't we leave that question? He wasn't on the scene at the time when my father and daughter disappeared.'

'It might be important. I need to know, if you can tell me.'

'Do I have to? I don't like talking about it.'

Slim took a deep breath. 'I heard a rumour. I'm sure it's just stupid but … I heard it was your father.'

Celia coughed, jerking the car again.

'Where'd you hear that?'

Slim shrugged. 'I was asking around. There were rumours you dropped out of school because you were pregnant. One of them was that Amos was the father.'

Celia gave a bitter laugh. 'I guess he could be, couldn't he?'

'What do you mean?'

Celia sighed. 'The truth is, I don't know who the father is. I've never known.'

28

THE LITTLE METRO SAT IN A LAYBY, OTHER CARS occasionally flashing past. Celia was on her third cigarette, while Slim, who had felt it polite to keep her company, was teasing down a Marlboro, wishing she preferred Lights to Reds.

'I used to wash dishes in the Crown in Penleven,' she said. 'Mother was always against it, said the place was full of local riffraff, but I insisted. I just wanted to be out of that house sometimes. I was fifteen. The kitchens shut at eight back then and I usually got let out about half nine. Sometimes I'd stop into the bar for a drink with the regulars if there were any about. It was early March and a Wednesday, our quietest day of the week, and there was no one in the bar, so I just headed home. Sometimes a regular would give me a lift, but if not I just walked. I was halfway home, on the Penleven to Trelee road, when someone … jumped me.'

Slim closed his eyes. He listened to Celia's soft draws on the cigarette.

'I hit my head on the road,' Celia continued. 'The guy dragged me through this gate into a field and did what he wanted. I was dazed, I couldn't easily fight back. He held me down until he was finished, then he was gone. I staggered home, crying. I wanted to tell my parents but my dad was locked in his study, and one look at my mother's eyes and I knew I couldn't say anything. I knew what she thought of me.' Celia started to laugh. 'I was roughed up a bit, grazes down the side of my face. I think I told her I'd been hit by a car or something. She told me to go take a shower.'

'I don't know what to say.'

Celia flapped a hand at him. 'Don't say anything. I like that you're not saying anything. This is stuff I've told no one.'

They smoked in silence for a couple more minutes, Slim occasionally stifling a cough into his hand. He declined Celia's offer of another cigarette, watching as she lit another, intent, it appeared, on smoking through the entire packet.

'You must have had suspicions,' Slim said at last. 'It never got reported?'

'Do you know how many rapes go unreported?' Celia snapped. When Slim gave a half-shrug, more to acknowledge that she wasn't asking so much as offering to tell him whether he wanted to know or not, she added, 'Most of them. I'm this fifteen-year-old school kid with a mother who already thinks I'm a slut, and I wasn't about to give her the satisfaction. I was no angel,

Slim. I had a habit of sneaking the leftover wine off the trays of cleared plates when I took them down to the kitchen. Killed the boredom if I was half cut, you know? I'd had a couple of glasses' worth that night, it was dark, and after I hit my head, I wasn't sure what was going on. I knew I'd been raped, but I was no virgin, even then. I tried to forget about it, blocked it out however I could, figured I probably deserved it, that I ought to make sure to take a heavy torch or hold my keys like a knife next time. Figured it was because I was young and stupid, but the memory would fade if I let it.' She sighed. 'Then I found out I was expecting Charlotte.'

'You're sure she was a result of the rape?'

Celia gave a bitter laugh. 'Jesus, Slim, I wasn't some back alley hooker. I had boyfriends, but I knew about safe sex. I'm certain she was a result of the rape.'

'Sorry,' Slim said. 'I'm used to dealing with insurance frauds and suspected affairs. It could be vital information, though. What you remember about the man.'

Celia started up the car and pulled back out on to the road. 'Look, we'd better get a shift on if your landlady's the miser you say she is. There's more to tell you, Slim. A lot more.'

They drove in silence for a while until they reached the Penleven turning. Celia scowled at the first sight of the sign, reeling off a string of swear words that reminded Slim of his Armed Forces days. He was beginning to like Celia. She was like a dying warrior; despite all the beatings life had thrown at her, she still had one knee off the ground, her sword arm raised, a defiant glare on her face as an unstoppable horde bore down on her.

'I hated this little hole,' she said. 'It's like Cornwall's cesspit.'

'I've found it quietly pleasant,' Slim said.

'You ought to have grown up here. Every farmer and his dog knew your business. My back would burn from the heat of eyes on it.'

'Do you think it was someone from the village who raped you?'

Celia said nothing. Slim wished he could take back his question, but at the same time wondered what he could assume from her silence. Finally, she pulled into a layby for passing cars a short distance from the village outskirts.

'I'll be in touch,' she said, then handed him a bag. 'Here. I thought these might be more useful than me telling you.'

He glanced inside the bag at a pair of VHS tapes.

'Home videos,' she said. 'My father and Charlotte. Have a watch on your own, see what you make of them.'

'Thanks.'

He climbed out. Celia pulled off without waiting for a goodbye, accelerating away as though desperate to get through Penleven as quickly as possible. Long after her lights had disappeared, he could still hear the strained growl of the Metro's engine as Celia jerked through the gears like an aggressive drunk on a test drive.

Slim stared at the bag in his hand. Then, with a sigh, he headed for the guesthouse.

29

Mrs. Greyson had upgraded to a DVD player, but the TV was an old tube one with a built in VCR. Slim slid the first tape into the slot then sat on the edge of the bed as the old TV flickered while warming up.

A grainy image of a farm appeared, static crisscrossing the screen, causing the picture to jump and jerk at odd intervals. A girl's voice Slim recognised as a young Celia was narrating a monologue about the moor as the camera swung around, and he could imagine it had been recently bought and only just removed from its packaging. This was the test run, the experiment to see how it worked.

The camera panned again. A woman sitting in a wheelchair someway off appeared, but the camera jerked quickly past her, bringing into shot a tall man with a child in his arms. The child, shoulder-length hair curled neatly inwards in a tidy bob, seemed reluctant to look at the camera, her head turned into the man's shoulder, her eyes downcast. The man, though, tall and wiry with a downward-pointing triangular face and close-cropped hair, stared directly into the lens and smiled. He lifted the hand not supporting the child and gave a quick wave.

'Hey, Dad.'

Amos Birch smiled then patted the girl on the shoulder. He opened his mouth to say something then snapped it shut as the fuzzy rattle of wheels on stone announced the approach of the wheelchair. The camera dropped to show a close-up of cobblestones as a voice said, 'Put that stupid thing away. Where'd you get it anyway?'

'Not now, Mum,' came a tired voice, and the view abruptly cut off.

Maybe hours or days had passed, but the view appeared again, this time of a closed outhouse door. Slim recognised it as the same door that still stood locked at Worth Farm.

'Dad?' came Celia's voice, followed by an amused chuckle. 'What are you working on today?'

The door swung open, and despite the graininess of the old camcorder image, Slim marveled at the grotto revealed within. It looked like a less colourful Santa's toy factory. Pieces of wood filled every available space, clock parts and half-finished sculptures hanging from strings tied around ceiling crossbeams. And despite the fuzz of the old recording, the sound of ticking was unmistakable. Coming from dozens of clocks at once, it was like the roosting of a hive of mechanical bees.

Amos Birch sat with his back to the door on a

wooden chair that was slightly too low for him. His spindly grasshopper's legs were bent, knees in the air, back hunched as he leaned over a worktop. The little girl sat close by, on the worktop with her legs dangling down, stock-still, her face turned to watch her grandfather at work. One hand rested on the work top, the other lay across her lap.

Neither initially noticed Celia, but as she took a few steps closer, Amos half-turned, folded a piece of paper he had been writing on and slid it into a drawer. The little girl didn't move, but Amos twisted on his chair to look up at his daughter. A frown followed by a frustrated look crossed his face.

'Celia. What are you doing in here? I'd prefer it if you could knock.'

It was the first time Slim had heard Amos Birch's voice. He frowned, trying not to read too much into a single utterance, yet recalled training he had undergone during his years in the Armed Forces for dealing with prisoners, and with hostage negotiations. Slim had never taken part in a real action, but remembered some of the information his instructor had taught about voice inflection, tremolo, and the authority with which an utterance was made. His immediate assessment of Amos Birch was that this was a shy man who preferred his own company and dealt poorly with stressful situations, struggling with social contact, even that involving his own family. As the tape continued with Celia entering the workroom and pointing the video camera over her father's shoulder at the pieces of a clock he had hastily pulled towards him, every movement Amos made only reinforced Slim's opinion.

This was a man who preferred to be left alone.

Was it any wonder then that he had got up one day and walked out of his workshop, never to return?

The main question Slim needed to answer now was why he had taken his granddaughter with him.

30

SLIM AWOKE TO KNOCKING ON HIS BEDROOM DOOR. He sat up, dazed, looked around and found he was lying crossways over his bed, the fuzz of the TV still buzzing after the video tape had finished and switched off.

He didn't remember how far he had got into the last tape before falling asleep, but he had been so engrossed in the gentle home videos of the Birches' family life that he'd continued watching well into the small hours. Now he had a sleep-deprived hangover worse than many he'd had on the bottle, and rubbed his eyes as he stumbled to the door.

'Mr. Hardy, are you in there?' Mrs. Greyson called through the door. 'A package arrived for you.'

He opened the door to find her holding something large with both hands. It was irregularly shaped and wrapped untidily with packing tape.

Mrs. Greyson looked Slim up and down with a mixture of revulsion and distrust. She held out the package then snapped, 'My house is not a postal service, Mr. Hardy. If you plan to have regular deliveries, may I suggest you set up a post office box in the village? I'm sure Mrs. Waite would enjoy the pleasure of your regular visits.'

'Thanks,' he said, taking it from her, surprised at its weight. He put it down on the floor as Mrs. Greyson closed the door and stumped back down the stairs, muttering in that loud but inaudible way he was now familiar with. Turning back to the dressing table, he picked up the sheet of paper he had scribbled notes on the night before.

Ask Celia about the letters. Who is he writing to?
Did she talk to his materials suppliers?
What's the logo at 37.23?
Is there any footage of Celia or Mary with Charlotte?
Why's the girl so well-behaved? Discipline or disability?

The list went on, another half a dozen items to consider, most of which he doubted would amount to much of interest. It was all background, angles and aspects to help build a portrait of Amos Birch, but it was unlikely to lead to clues as to his whereabouts or final resting place unless Slim got lucky.

There had to be more, Slim thought, as he hauled the package up on to the bed, frowning at its weight. What had Alan sent him? He'd never known a lock pick to weigh so much, but when he ripped the package open, he understood.

'You old bastard,' Slim muttered, unable to resist a smile.

Rather than take Slim's request seriously, Alan had opted to play a practical joke, the kind he might have down back at Harrogate: shaving part of Slim's shoelaces so they broke during a march, or filling his boots with chili powder.

The package's contents would deal with a padlock, all right.

Alan had sent him a pair of police-grade bolt cutters.

After apologising for the delivery's inconvenience, Slim had Mrs. Greyson make him a sandwich, which she did with a grumbling reluctance even though he offered to pay. Taking just the sandwich and a fold-up rain mac, he headed out for a stroll around the village, needing to clear his head, to give himself time to think. As he reached the shop, a figure bustled out, bumping into him.

'Sorry!' A pause. 'Oh, it's you.'

'June.'

She looked no better in daylight than she did under the pub's gloomy lighting. As though aware he was appraising her, she tucked a strand of hair behind her ear and rubbed at a blemish on her cheek.

'I was wondering what happened to you. It's been a few days. Looks like you've been in the wars.'

For a moment Slim thought she meant literally then he remembered the bruises that were now beginning to fade.

'Pretty easy to hurt yourself on Bodmin Moor,' he said. 'Rocks sticking up all over the place.'

She nodded, but as she made to push past him, he added, 'Do you want to get a coffee? Is there somewhere round here you can do that?'

June looked at him as though he'd just stepped off a plane in a foreign land. 'Where do you think this is, Plymouth?'

They ended up sitting on a tattered bench with one rotten leg on a patch of wild verge where the Camelford and Launceston roads intersected, drinking two cans of Coke bought from the shop. June, in a skirt, sat awkwardly forward, as though afraid that the long grass reclaiming the bench's feet hid rats and other nasties. Slim, who had lived alongside plenty of worse things during his years in the Armed Forces, sat back and enjoyed the view through a gateway opposite the cluster of houses surrounding the church, which made up Penleven's core.

'I'm trying to find out what happened to Amos Birch,' Slim said. 'I guess there's no point hiding it. I'm not sure whether it's something I can figure out, but I plan to try.'

June sighed. 'Before my time, was Amos. Ninety-five he disappeared?'

'Ninety-six.'

'Yeah, see, I didn't move here til oh-two.'

'No?'

June gave a bitter laugh. Slim said nothing, waiting for the story to come.

'I'm from another nowhere just off the A30 near

Saltash. Den—my husband—was a traveling salesman. Insurance. He might have been Superman for all I cared. We got hitched, moved here.' She shrugged. 'House was cheap. Bit of a dead end, but I liked it. It was all right at first but we weren't here a year before Den started to change. I wondered if there was something in the water. He started getting short-tempered, had no time for me, was always off fishing down the Camel estuary with his mates or hanging out in the bookies in Camelford when he wasn't on the road. I got the job in the Crown to get out of his way of an evening because I got tired of the arguments over stupid little things. Wasn't no surprise when he went off somewhere and didn't come back.'

'He disappeared?'

June laughed. 'No, no such mystery there. He had another woman up near Bristol. He'd been staying with her on business trips since before we moved down here, then one day he just moved in for good. I got a phone call one day to say he wasn't coming back, but to be honest, I wasn't all that surprised. I had savings from my old dad's passing, so I bought him out of the house. Good riddance. Been alone in there ever since, but you know, you get used to it.'

Slim sensed it would only take a word to receive a home-visit invite, but he resisted the call of his own seeping loneliness.

'So you don't know much about the Birch family?'

Just the rumours. 'They all came out again around the time of Mary's passing back in oh-six.' She smiled. 'I worked in the pub, you know.'

'I can guess,' Slim said. 'Tell me what you know about Celia.'

'The Birch girl? Well, I call her a girl but she wouldn't be much younger than me. Heard she lives off over Tavistock way.'

Slim gave a non-committal shrug.

'By my time she wasn't round these parts much. Holed up nursing that old mother of hers through her last days, I suppose. I never saw her close up, just at a distance a couple of times. Soon as Mary passed and the farm was sold off, she was gone for good. I think she got tired of this place. Vipers' pits of rumours, these little villages. And she had a reputation.'

'What reputation?'

'Well, I don't like to tell tales—', here Slim gave a vehement shake of the head while hiding a smile, '—but in her youth she put it about a bit. Worked in the pub, she did, and rumour had it she was anyone's around closing. Especially if you'd not gone with her before. Not a man in the village who didn't go with young Celia at some point, so they say.'

'So she was kind of the village bike?'

June gave a nervous laugh. 'Yeah, I don't like to say it, but that would be about the best description. Can't blame her, really, not much else to do round here.' As though figuring she might as well try her luck, she put a hand on Slim's thigh. 'Chance would be a fine thing.'

Certain a couple of drinks would make it possible, Slim cooled the temptation by remembering the potential aftermath.

'I have PTSD,' he said.

June snapped her hand away. 'Oh, like from the war? You're not one of those guys who goes psycho, are you?'

Slim smiled. 'No. Not from the war, from my last girlfriend. She tried to kill me.'

'I won't ask.'

'Don't.'

After an awkward moment in which they both sipped their Cokes, Slim said, 'But Michael came along and calmed Celia down?'

'So I heard. They were a couple for a while and it got serious. Then Amos pulled a runner and Celia broke it off. After that, she withdrew and you hardly ever saw her. I mean, it's probably not as sinister as it sounds. She was nineteen, I heard, when Amos left. She was probably working in Plymouth. Turned her back on Penleven, had enough of the rumours and the small-town mentality. It's easy to do. I mean, she lived over in Trelee. As easy to pop into Camelford for groceries as to come down here. Plenty of people round here who don't take any part in the community. I guess they all have real lives.'

'What do you think happened?'

'Me? To Amos?' June laughed. 'I think he went off with some woman,' she said. 'I mean, why wouldn't he? He was what, mid-fifties? Not too old to start again, is it, if you've got a dragon at home. Daughter's old enough to lead her own life. And, I mean, it's not like he wouldn't have had the chance, is it? I heard his clocks were worth thousands, and he could fix anything. Heard he used to fix the beat up old thing over the pub bar, got it running when it hadn't run in years. Stopped again now, though.'

Slim smiled. 'What about Mary? She was in a wheelchair, wasn't she?'

June gave a dismissive flap of her hand. 'Ah, he could have got her a home help if he was feeling guilty, could have left her a bit of his fortune and then just got on with it. She got the farm, after all, didn't she?'

'But to just vanish like that?'

'I heard he wasn't one for confrontation.'

'Would someone who didn't like confrontation do something as drastic as run off with another woman? Wouldn't he have stayed put, kept it secret?'

June smiled. 'You're quite the fantasist, aren't you?'

'I'm worse after a few drinks.'

June laughed. Rubbing her arm against the chilly breeze, she stood up. 'I'm afraid, Slim, that I have to go get ready for work. It's been a pleasure talking to you. I hope you show up in the pub again sometime soon. And if you ever fancy a nightcap … I make great tea.'

Slim was about to wave her goodbye when a thought came to mind. He reached into his pocket and withdrew a small notebook. 'It can get lonely up at that guesthouse,' he said. 'Can you write me your address, just in case I really want that tea?'

June cocked her head, a hint of colour in her cheeks. 'What's this, your little black book?'

Slim shrugged. 'The cover's blue.'

'A clever disguise.' June scribbled down her address then tucked the pen suggestively into her blouse before pulling it out and handing it back. 'I'll keep my back door off the latch just in case. Quite fancy me a night stalker.'

They shared an awkward smile as though unsure how much of their conversation was jest, then June nodded.

'I've really got to go, Slim.'

Slim nodded. 'Your husband was a fool, June. I'm already looking forward to my next pint of pisswater and the pleasure of your company.'

June smiled, then turned and walked away, not looking back. Slim watched her until she was out of sight, pondering her words. So much rumour. He was certain the truth was in there somewhere, like a caged animal fighting to get out.

31

IT WAS JUST AFTER SEVEN WHEN THE DOOR OF THE middle terrace opened and Michael appeared, still buttoning up a dress shirt under the unzipped jacket he wore. As he reached the gate that opened onto the road, Slim stood up straight from where he had been leaning against the waist-high stone wall that fronted the three council houses.

'Hey, Michael,' he said. 'I was wondering if you could help me. It's Friday, right? If I wanted to hit a club, would it be better to go to Camelford or Bude?'

Michael stared at him with his brow bunched into a frown. 'Are you stalking me? How did you know where I live?'

'Not hard when people are so willing to talk,' Slim said as Michael came through the gate and walked up to him. It made him feel bad to admit it, but something about Michael got under his skin. Michael had the fading good looks of a former boyband singer two decades past his sell-by date, with the physique of a man who could handle himself in a bar fight. Slim, who had enjoyed his share of punch-ups during his army service, wondered how a ruck between them would end, and chided himself for feeling tempted to find out.

'What do you want from me?'

'Tell me about Celia and you.'

Michael gritted his teeth. 'You've got a nerve—'

Slim lifted a hand. 'Save it. I'm working for someone who wants Amos Birch found. You don't have to talk to me, but if you have nothing to hide it won't hurt, will it?'

Michael shook his head. 'You don't need to go dredging all this up. You're going to upset a lot of people talking about the Birches. As far as people around here are concerned, that's old news.'

'Why? If you've got nothing to hide, why does it matter?'

Michael came a couple of steps closer, but Slim held his ground.

'I'm warning you,' Michael said. 'Get out of my way.'

'You know what I think?' Slim said, standing up straighter, letting the remnants of his army stature do the imposing for him. 'I think you knocked him off. I think he objected to you and Celia. I think you were an angry young man who thought he could do anything and get away with it.' At Michael's incredulous look, he added, 'I'm not saying it was intentional. Perhaps words got a little heated, and you blew your top. You hit him with something heavy. It happens. Believe me, I know.'

'You don't know anything,' Michael snapped.

'That's why I'm standing here. Come on, Michael. Where's the body?'

'What body? I didn't kill him!'

'So why did Celia blame you for his disappearance?'

Michael lifted a closed fist, and for a few seconds Slim thought, *here we go, here's the fight I've been baiting him for,* then Michael turned and swung at open air. A couple more air punches and a howl of frustration, and he slumped, leaning on the fence, head bowed.

'You won't leave it, will you?'

Slim felt quietly relieved. His face still felt fragile from the drunken dustup in Plymouth, and Michael's air-punches looked like they would hurt.

'Tell me what you know. That's all.'

Michael gritted his teeth as though about to scream. Instead, he said, 'I asked her to marry me. That's all. She was the only girl I've ever wanted. And guess what? Miracle of miracles, she said yes. Then that bastard had to go and walk away. She broke it off, literally cut me off dead. We weren't even friends anymore. I had the police around, questioning me. She blamed me, she had to have. I mean, what was I supposed to think?'

'She told you it was your fault?'

Michael looked up. Tears shone in his eyes, and Slim felt a pang of regret. 'I've spoken to her exactly once since the day I asked her to marry me. She said I was a mistake. We were a mistake.'

'And you just let it go?'

'Of course not. But next thing I know, I've got police at the door. I was their number one suspect. I got held for three days, had them practically squeezing a confession out of me. That cooled me a little, and by the time I was let go, I'd lost my nerve. Sure, I tried to contact her. I went round there, but she'd gone, off to college somewhere. I saw her at a distance from time to time, but I could never get close, and I was scared, you know?'

'Scared they'd try to pin something on you?'

'I was twenty years old at the time. I thought I loved Celia, but the idea of being banged up for the rest of my life for murder … no thanks.'

'But without a body—'

'One could have shown up. How was I supposed to know that twenty odd years later he'd still be missing?'

'So what did you do?'

'What do you think? I kept my head down, my mouth shut, and I tried not to think about … her.'

Slim nodded. 'So you asked her to marry you, yeah? Why Celia? I've heard she was a little … loose.'

Michael shrugged. 'People can say what they want about her. It was all lies. Celia was a good person caught up in a bad situation.'

Slim frowned. 'Tell me about this bad situation.'

Michael rubbed his eyes and shook his head. 'I don't have time for any of this. I left it alone a long time ago. Why'd you have to come around digging this up?'

'Like I said, someone wants to know what happened to Amos Birch.'

'Who?'

'I'm sorry, but right now I can't tell you that. Maybe in time, if I get anywhere. Answer me one more question. Do you think Celia could have killed him? You know, something like ninety percent of murders are done by a relative or close friend—'

Michael gave a bitter laugh. 'Don't quote statistics at me. I watch the same crime documentaries that you do. No, I don't think she killed him. I thought she loved me, but she idolised her father. He was everything to her. Now, I could totally believe she knocked off her mother. That woman was a dragon in a metal chair.'

'Mary?'

'Yeah. She ruled Celia like a dictator, had a whip over her back.'

'She beat her?'

Michael waved his hand again. 'Oh, I don't know if she meant literally. Celia said it was all about image. Keeping up an appearance for her father's reputation, and that Celia was shaming the family by not being better at school, not being a perfect daughter. For his part, he didn't seem to care as long as he was left alone with his machines.'

'Clocks?'

'That's what he sold, but he made all sorts, I've heard. Wind-up toys, that kind of thing. Mechanical stuff. Things he built and sold off to specialist collectors overseas. The man was a magician with his hands. In Penleven he was a legend when I was growing up, the kind of guy whose house you'd walk past and be like, 'that's where that guy lives'. I mean, how was Celia supposed to live up to that?'

'So you can understand her behavior?'

'She went with a couple of guys, whatever. Not like

most of us wouldn't play the field if we had a chance. Weren't you ever a teenager?'

Slim nodded. 'Once. Drank my way through it.'

'I liked her because she didn't give a damn what people thought of her. Free spirit, that kind of thing. Girl like that shouldn't have looked twice at a guy like me, but she did, and I wasn't about to let that go.'

'What you said about her mother … what did you mean by that?'

'Mary Birch was a tyrant. She had MS, and made sure everyone she met knew what an inconvenience it was, and how the whole world was responsible. To be quite honest, from the way Celia described her and from what I saw, I'm surprised old Amos lasted so long. Someone should have put a knife in the old crone's back years before he ran off.'

32

SLIM STARED AT THE WAD OF PRINTOUTS IN HIS HAND as he turned out of the guesthouse entrance, thinking both that it was time to discuss costs with Celia and to think about hiring a secretary.

For once it was a clear day with a bright overhead sun, even though the air had turned cold. Slim walked up through the village and took the Trelee road, waiting until he got to the bench on the verge near Worth Farm. He sat down, smiled at the view over Bodmin Moor, then got to work.

Company information on every watch- or clockmaker he could find online, vast reams of information on the process of watch- and clock-making, the types of materials used, as well as anything he could find on Amos Birch: online sales listings, reviews, promotional material. There was less than he'd hoped, but still far more than he could get through in a couple of hours. It was the kind of trawling, needle-in-a-haystack clue-hunting drudge work an incident room team would assign to its junior officers. Slim wondered absently if June would be interested in a career change: she had the kind of face that would scare off irate customers, and if he showed off enough of his incredible detective skills he could instill in her the kind of adulation his fragile confidence needed.

He gave a wry smile. Wishful thinking, but nope. He was a one-man band, and the heavy lifting was his chore alone.

As he began to read, he realised he wasn't sure what he was even looking for. Instead, he simply let his mind drift, waiting for something to stand out.

An hour later, he put down his pen and stared off through the leaves of the trees backing on to Worth Farm's lower side, to the hills of Bodmin Moor beyond. The Amos Birch case was a tangled mess, and he was aching for a drink.

To put his mind off the temptation, he climbed over the stile and walked down through the field to the gurgling stream at the back of Worth Farm, keeping an eye out for the farm's aggressive owner as he did so. A line of gnarled trees about ten metres high overhung the hedge lining the farm's lower slope, their upper branches bent by the incessant wind to make the muddy bank down to the stream into a tunnel. Slim's footing was uncertain, at the mercy of loose clods of peat and hidden rocks until he reached the far end, where the line of trees became abruptly less encroaching, as though the two halves of the row had been planted at generational intervals. These shorter trees were more spaced apart than the others, almost ordered.

Slim frowned. They were only just budding with spring leaves, but he found a couple of dried fallen ones lying on the ground. He picked them up and stuffed them into his pocket.

Back at the guesthouse, he knocked on Mrs. Greyson's living room door. He was answered with a groggy 'come in,' and opened the door to find her watching an old *Cheers* rerun on Channel Four with a glass of amber liquid in her hand. The urge to snatch the brandy and drink it himself was so strong Slim took a step back. Taking a deep breath, he concentrated on the old clock ticking lethargically on the mantel, each second such a shuddering labour it seemed set to quit at any moment. It read a little after three, which surprised Slim, who thought it was a lot later.

'Don't mind that, it's slow,' Mrs. Greyson said, noticing his gaze. 'It never has run on time. Can I help you with something, Mr. Hardy? I'm guessing this isn't a social visit?'

'I wondered if you had a book on wildlife I could borrow? Flowers and plants?'

Mrs. Greyson sighed. 'Do I look like a librarian?' Before Slim could answer that she did indeed resemble one every bit as much as a guesthouse owner, she flapped a hand at a bookshelf beside the TV. 'There's one there. That tall one with the white spine. The hardback.'

'Thanks.'

With Mrs. Greyson's disapproving gaze following him, Slim took the book and went up to his room.

The leaves he had picked up off the ground were in such a state of decay it was hard to tell what their original shape had been, but by a process of deducting all the leaves they definitely weren't, Slim became quietly confident that the trees backing onto Worth Farm were lime trees.

From the genus *tallia*, lime trees were known in Germany as linden trees, where they were commonly used for the construction of cuckoo clocks, their wood being light and easily carved. Even though the incessant moorland wind had distorted their distinctive pyramidal shape, it was clear that Amos had planted the trees to create his own supply.

But, with the lime trees being a hardwood, and therefore with a slow growth rate of a foot or two per year, Amos must have known it would be decades before they were large enough for the wood to be useable. Slim estimated that the shorter trees were in the region of twenty-five years old, meaning Amos had planted them not long before his disappearance, banking on them becoming a long-term materials supply for his projects.

Slim allowed himself a small nod of satisfaction. It was a small break, but a break nonetheless.

'You planned to come back, didn't you?' he whispered, staring at a small pen picture he had found of Amos Birch on a clock review site. 'Wherever you went, you planned to come back.'

33

Plymouth had far more to offer than either Tavistock or Liskeard. After being told by the receptionist in the registrar's office that his request would take a couple of hours to process, Slim found his way up to Plymouth Hoe, where he resisted a sharp wind to gaze out at Drake's Sound. Far out in the English Channel, a couple of container ships moved on what looked like a collision course, the distances between them skewed by their relative sizes and the choppy expanse of grey water. Slim, dressed in a brand new jacket he felt becoming of his status as a private investigator and wearing a woolen beanie hat which definitely wasn't, only now understood the pervading sense of claustrophobia that came as standard in a tiny moorland village like Penleven. It was no wonder Celia had needed to escape. Each time he walked past the shop or the pub, he felt the draw of the booze on sale stronger than ever. Only the night before, after Mrs.

Greyson had gone to bed, he had sneaked downstairs, and, accompanied by the lethargically ticking clock, taken a bottle of brandy out of a cabinet in her living room and turned it over in his hands. Half full, everything about it had appealed: the sound of the liquid sloshing against the glass, the feel of the cap, the colour of the brandy … his hands had shook as he put it back. He had found the strength to turn and walk away, but it wouldn't be much longer before he cracked again. The ghost of Amos Birch was calling him, invisible fingernails scraping at his resolve.

He was meeting Celia again after lunch. She had cancelled their previous meeting due to unforeseen circumstances, perhaps to do with her job, although she hadn't specified. He wanted to give her good news, but aside from a few vague ideas, he had little to go on. Celia, he felt, held all the cards. Something she said would be the key, but he still couldn't clear her of suspicion. She was the centre of everything.

An hour later, back at the registrar's office, he picked up the document he had been waiting for—a copy of Mary Birch's death certificate. To his frustration there was nothing suspicious about it. Mary Birch, née Merrifield, born October 9th, 1949, had died of a urinary tract infection attributed to complications due to multiple sclerosis, on June 14th, 2006.

Slim pulled out his notebook and did all his customary checks, but there were no significant connections to any of the dates, and the cause of death was a common complication of her overreaching illness. He had also printed out some information about commonly available chemicals that could be adapted as poisons, but poison-related deaths were usually heart or respiratory failure.

It looked as though, for all the intrigue it would otherwise create, that Mary Birch had died a painful but otherwise mundane death.

Slim bought fish n' chips then headed for the harbour, where he was sitting on a bench and looking out to see when Celia arrived. She sat down heavily beside him, sighed, and immediately pulled out a cigarette.

'Sorry,' she said.

Unsure to what she was referring, Slim said, 'Busy day at work?'

Celia shrugged. 'Someone was sick.'

'I made a few enquiries,' Slim said. 'Nothing much to go on. I wondered if you could find a list of old employees at your father's farm. One of them might have seen something.'

'I doubt it,' Celia said.

'What about Michael?'

Celia's head snapped around. 'What about him?'

'I talked to him.'

Without a word, Celia stood up and began walking away. Slim thought for a moment that she was leaving, then she stopped, waved her hands as though shaking off water, turned and marched back, eyes wild.

'Don't go talking to people like that without asking me first.'

'Why not?'

'Because it's all lies. He doesn't know anything. He thought he knew me but he didn't know anything.'

'He loved you. He told me that. I think he still does.'

Celia turned away, and when she turned back, tears shone in her eyes.

'Don't taunt me, Slim. Don't taunt me with what I could have had. You don't know what happened. You don't know any of it.'

He wanted to shake her, but he forced his hands into his pockets where they had less chance of betraying him. 'Then tell me. I can't find your father unless you tell me what you know.'

Celia, sobbing, sat down on the bench. Slim handed her a tissue, feeling a little guilty that it had occupied the back pocket of his jeans for at least two weeks.

'I was only nineteen, I know,' Celia said. 'After everything that happened, I felt so much older. I'd not been with Michael all that long but I felt so sure about him. Something clicked between us, and when he asked … of course I said yes. I told my parents together, and my mother flew into such a rage … I was stunned. She called me every name under the sun. She called me a slut, told me I was crazy, no one would marry a nutjob like me. I told my father to take Charlotte out of there, so he went out to his workshop. He never liked our arguments and I could see that he was happy to leave. It was always me and Mother. I'd fight back until she ground me down, but my dad, he always wanted to get out of the way, and Charlotte rarely left his side. That was the last time I saw either of them.'

Slim nodded. 'So you think that's why he left?'

'Yes.'

'Your mother's anger drove your father to run off with Charlotte, and yet you blamed Michael? The man who loved you?'

'After my father disappeared, Michael became a suspect. It shames me to say it, but I suspected it too. You see, he was waiting outside for me that night. I was going to call him in after I'd told them about our engagement, but I argued with my mother for hours, and when I finally walked out, I couldn't find him. He must have heard the shouting and run off. That was when I decided to find my father, because it was time to put Charlotte to bed. His workshop empty, both of them gone.'

Slim put up a hand. 'So, wait a minute. Michael was outside when your father disappeared?'

'Yes.'

'So he could have seen something.'

Celia shrugged. 'Sure, he could have done. When I spoke to him a couple of days later, he said he got tired of waiting and went home. He was interviewed by police but had nothing to tell them. To be honest, I wondered, but it was stupid to think it. Michael was a pub bruiser, but he wasn't the kind of guy to kill an old man and a child. He was rough on the outside but soft on the inside. That's why I liked him. In all the time we were together, he never so much as raised his voice to me.' Celia sniffed, wiping away a tear. 'And I used to get after him sometimes, too. With me he was a perfect gentleman.'

'He said you've only spoken once since he asked you to marry him.'

Celia waved a hand as though to dismiss the question. 'I called him to break it off a few days later. That's when he told me he went home.'

'But not right after?'

'I was angry. I blamed him for everything, and after my mother gave his name to the police, he was taken into custody. They had nothing on him but a loose motive, so he was released. My mother did her best to have him rearrested on multiple occasions claiming he had to be responsible in the absence of any other possibilities, but as time passed, and no sign of my father or Charlotte turned up, the case against him went cold. For me, though, it changed everything.'

'You associated Michael with your father and daughter's disappearance so you couldn't go back to the way you were before?'

Celia clicked her fingers. 'That's exactly it. You should be a counselor.'

Slim smiled. 'I've been told that before, but I get enough death threats in this line of work to risk getting any more. So Michael continued working at Worth Farm?'

'Ha, no way. My mother fired him. He never came back.'

Slim nodded slowly. He tried to picture the scene: a blazing argument, Amos Birch picking up a young girl and carrying her out of the room, but instead of taking the girl up to her bedroom, he went out to his workshop, and then out to the moor. With the girl in his arms, he walked halfway up Rough Tor, buried a clock in the peaty earth, then walked away, neither of them to be seen again.

No.

It was impossible.

'You said they found footprints,' he said.

'The police? Yes. So they told my mother.'

'But only one set? Your father carried your daughter? The whole way? It must have been hard for him. I mean, that clock I found is heavy, and a three-year-old child would weigh what, a couple of stone at least. In those videos he looks quite thin—'

'He was stronger than he looked,' Celia said. 'He was wiry rather than bulky, but farming work, and all his hobbies … they took a lot more effort than you might think.'

'But to carry her and that clock—'

'Look, I don't know how he did it. Perhaps someone snatched Charlotte and he went after her.'

'Do you really think so?'

Celia shrugged, then fixed Slim with a hard glare. 'If I knew the answers, I wouldn't be here talking to you, would I?'

Before Slim could reply, Celia abruptly looked at her watch. She gave a little shake of her head as though the time itself was frustrating for her, before standing up, simultaneously pulling a cigarette out of her pocket. She waved it around in the air as though the wind itself could light it, then said, 'I have to go. Keep in touch. And thanks, Slim.'

'I haven't done anything yet.'

'But you will, I'm sure of it.'

As he watched her walk away, Slim frowned. Celia was like a pressure valve being flexed, letting out information in sudden rushes, but keeping a lot hidden inside. It was too early to make her a suspect, but if there was anyone to suspect, it was Celia.

34

IN AN ATTEMPT TO AVOID INVOKING MRS. GREYSON'S wrath yet again, Slim pulled a rain-soaked business card out of his wallet and dialed what was left of the Lakeview's number, leaving a message on an automated voicemail to say he was staying overnight in Plymouth. Then he wandered about until he found a cheap hostel near the Hoe, taking a private basement room.

The library opened later than the last buses ran, and also contained a far greater newspaper archive. After getting a sandwich and an espresso for dinner, Slim searched a computer database for Amos's name then refined the search by date to pinpoint the articles dealing with the investigation. This time he was after specific information and he got it.

Mentioned in several articles was a significant police-led search of the surrounding moorland. And in each case it was noted that nothing of interest was found.

Bodmin Moor was a sizable place, but it was no

Dartmoor or Lake District. That a casual hiker had failed to turn up the buried clock in the last twenty years was feasible, but that a full police investigation had turned up nothing?

Unlikely. Slim shook his head. More like impossible.

Which left him with an unusual possibility: that the clock and the letter hidden inside it had been buried at a later date, after the search had concluded.

Either Amos Birch had returned to do it, or someone else had.

Someone who likely knew about his whereabouts after his disappearance.

There was something else that kept recurring too: the name of a detective inspector linked to the case, Mark Cassell. On a whim, Slim consulted a phone book and found only three Cassells with an M initial. The first call was answered by a lady who accused him of wanting to sell her something, but the second by a gruff voice who confirmed he was a retired police officer and agreed to meet him.

Unexpectedly, Slim found himself in a pub near the harbour, sitting opposite a man in his seventies whose stern features and hard eyes left no doubt to his former profession. With an Alsatian lying with its head over the man's feet which growled every time Slim met its eyes, he had taken a sip of the pint already bought for him before he could think what he was doing.

'You're a journalist, are you?'

'Documentary filmmaker,' Slim said, using the old alias. 'I'm trying to assess the possibility of a film on the disappearance of Amos Birch—'

Cassell flapped a hand. 'You said on the phone. You'd be wasting your time.'

'You were the investigator in charge?'

'I was indeed. The man ran out on his wife. That's about it. Happens all the time. It was only so high profile because he was well-known and he left no trace, but it got more attention and used more police resources than it deserved.'

'You're sure he ran off?'

'Absolutely. And it was hard to blame him. I sat through several interviews with his wife, and she was as ghastly a human being as I've ever met. And I don't mean just the way she looked—she was no oil painting, believe me—but everything about her. She swore worse than we did in the academy, she had nothing good to say about anyone, and she treated his disappearance as a business issue rather than a personal thing.'

'What do you mean?'

'He was a minor celebrity, and she liked the wealth that came with it. Their house was full of junk, all sorts of rubbish she was buying off the TV and online, back when it was a new thing to do that. She told us she'd kill him for real when we tracked him down. Showed no concern for his welfare other than how it might reflect on her.'

'You don't think there's a chance she was responsible for his murder?'

Cassell laughed. 'Not a chance. Even had she been physically capable, it would have defied all motive. She simply had no reason to kill him.'

Hardly aware of his actions but regretting every

step, Slim found himself at the bar, ordering a second round of drinks. When he sat back down he said, 'What about the daughter?'

'Celia Birch? She wasn't much better. Seduced one of the junior officers. He had to be disciplined. Nearly lost his job, but we'd have been screwed if there was a case to be made. Compromised witness and all that.'

Slim gaped. 'She slept with one of the police on the case?'

'The girl was loose, let's put it that way. And not in her right mind. She was rambling, barely legible. We had to use special liaison officers to interview her. One of the trainees got too close.'

'But there was no suspicion of her?'

'Of course there was. We considered that she and the boyfriend were in on it together, but again, no motive, no evidence. Had they knocked off the mother, it would have been different. We could tell there was plenty of friction there, but between the dad and the girl … by all accounts, they were close. Like, he was the last person she would have knocked off. That doesn't mean it didn't happen, of course not. But ninety-nine times out of a hundred? No way.'

'And the boyfriend was cleared? I heard he was a suspect.'

'Mostly because he lied. He said he was at home that night. She told us he was waiting outside. Either way, once he'd broken down and confessed to getting scared, we had nothing on him. No motive, no evidence.'

The Alsatian looked up and gave a soft bark, as though to confirm what the old policeman claimed.

'I heard a rumour Celia had a child,' Slim said tentatively, not sure how much he ought to reveal. 'And that Amos Birch took the child when he left.'

'A lot of rumours surrounded that family,' Cassell said. 'I heard nothing about a child during the investigation. It was for a single missing person, not two. If it were, it would be something to consider.'

'If I had proof, would it make a difference?' Slim asked, thinking of the videos and their grainy images of Amos Birch carrying Charlotte in his arms. He had sent one to Kay for analysis, but the others were hidden under his mattress. Celia had asked for her keepsakes back, but Slim had so far managed to stall her.

'I'm long retired, but I have colleagues in the force who were young when that case happened. They'd be interested, I'm sure. Like I said, there was no evidence of a child. None registered to the address, and no sign one had ever lived there. We conducted a search of the house during the investigation, but aside from a whole lot of junk … nothing.'

'So there was nothing suspicious at all?'

Cassell leaned forward. 'To me, only the delay.'

'What delay?'

'Birch was gone nearly two full days before his disappearance was reported. The mother explained it away as saying he did that sometimes, wandered off to be alone. No proof, so of course we did a forensics sweep, seeing as they'd have had time to clean up. But a crazy teenager and a woman in a wheelchair? They'd have left something. Nope, not a thing. And Celia and her boyfriend hadn't even aligned their stories. We had nothing to go on. Only the prints of a man's shoes in the mud on the path down towards the moor, a man walking away.'

'And no one local saw anything?'

'We interviewed, of course. Birch was an enigmatic but well-liked man. Not well-known on a personal level, it seemed, although he had a few customers in the area for whom he fixed old clocks from time to time. One or two were quite upset to hear of his disappearance, but no one had seen him.'

Slim took a sip of his beer, aware there were now three empty glasses beside him to Cassell's two.

'So you think it was an open and shut case? Nothing to suggest foul play at all?'

Cassell leaned forward, then slowly rose to his feet, as though it took much effort. 'I'll leave you my number, if this miraculous new evidence comes to light, but I know what you want. You TV people are all the same. You're fishing for a mystery that just isn't there. More than five hundred people go missing each year in Devon and Cornwall alone. Most of them are never heard of again. Were they all murdered? Some, for sure. But most?' He gave a tired shake of his head. 'I'll bid you good evening, sir.'

Slim stood up to watch him leave, the dog padding quietly at Cassell's side. Then he sat down and took a long swig of his beer, sighing as he did so.

Another nothing lead. He ought to go back to his hostel, make some notes, get some rest, but he was already drunk.

Might as well have another beer.

35

Mrs. Greyson looked like a storm had come clattering through and left its impression on her face.

'I don't appreciate my guesthouse being used as a drop-in centre,' she snapped. 'If you have cause to just come and go as you please then I suggest you find somewhere else for the remainder of your stay.'

'I called you … I left you a message.'

'No, Mr. Hardy, you didn't call me.' A stern finger pointed at the phone on the table in the hall. 'Do you see a flashing light? No, neither do I. No messages. Had you not been a full grown man I might have called the police.'

Slim frowned, trying to order his thoughts through a blistering hangover. He was sure he had called her. He fumbled with his phone in his pocket, determined to check, but succeeded only in dropping it on the doormat, among a handful of letters addressed to Mrs. Greyson. He scrambled for it, but his hands were shaking. He was yet to have a drink since passing out last night and waking up by some miracle in the hostel room he had rented. Another nine hours of resistance, another futile sand fort which would eventually, inevitably be breached and overrun by the relentless tide. By the time his uncooperative fingers had opened the recent calls log to discover he had inadvertently left a voicemail on a number which missed by three digits the large print, highlighted number pinned to the wall above the guesthouse's phone, Mrs. Greyson had swooped under him to rescue her post from the muddy dangers of his stumbling feet.

'What's going on with you, Mr. Hardy?' Mrs. Greyson said, stepping back with her letters clutched tightly against her chest.

For the first time, Slim detected a hint of sympathy. 'I'm caught up in a nasty web and I can't get out,' Slim said, shoving his hands into his pockets to hide the shaking, even though Mrs. Greyson had already seen. 'I'm doing everything I can, but every time I think I've escaped, I get caught up again.'

Mrs. Greyson sighed. 'Sometimes it's not possible to escape,' she said, looking down at her feet. 'Sometimes you have to learn to live with your captivity.' Then, offering a rare smile, she added, 'Would a coffee help? I know how to make the kind that might.'

Slim nodded. 'Thanks. If it's not too much trouble.'

Mrs. Greyson lifted an eyebrow. 'Is there anything that isn't trouble about you, Mr. Hardy?'

Slim could only shrug. He opened his mouth to respond, then closed it again and shook his head.

'Well, I've cleared up the breakfast things,' Mrs. Greyson said, 'but it's a nice enough day, so if you'd like to sit on the back veranda…?'

'Sure.'

She led him through the dining room with its empty tables and out a pair of patio doors onto a rear deck overlooking a neat garden. Tidy flowerbeds lined a lawn leading down a gentle slope to a cluster of trees backing on to a hedge that separated the garden from the adjacent farmland. Slim waited while Mrs. Greyson went back inside, then returned with two coffees in petit china cups. A sip of the scalding liquid confirmed she had laced it with brandy.

'I'm afraid there isn't much colour in the garden at this time of year,' she said. 'We're a week or two away from the daffodils. They always seem to come later here than you see on the BBC Weather reports. It's like Penleven has been forgotten in more ways than one.'

'It's pretty,' Slim said. 'It must be hard to maintain. You must be busy, looking after the guesthouse as well.'

'I've always been used to it,' she said. 'Even before my husband passed.'

'Oh, I'm sorry to hear that. How long has it been?'

'Not long enough,' Mrs. Greyson said with sudden vehemence. 'My Roy … he had one face for the outside, and one for the in.'

Slim said nothing. He stared at the line of trees, his coffee cup held protectively in his hands. The brandy was already doing its job, calming his nerves, slowing his heart. In the place of its fading apprehension came a slowly creeping guilt that yet again he had failed.

'He drove a lorry,' Mrs. Greyson said, her gaze far away, lost in the fields. 'He'd be away a few days at a time, sometimes a week or more. When he was at home … I needed to self-medicate from time to time. So I know how it feels. You know, what you're dealing with. More than just time to time, I'd say. More like all the time.'

Slim closed his eyes. 'I'm sorry.'

'Don't be. I got used to it over the years. It's funny how things change, isn't it? I can still remember our wedding day, and the years afterwards when we were happy. Later events might have soiled the memories somewhat, but I still knew genuine happiness. For a time. But we shouldn't be greedy, should we?'

She lifted her coffee and took a sip. A wince and a smile told Slim that Mrs. Greyson had added a little self-medication to her own, too.

'I guess not,' Slim said. 'When did he, um, pass?'

'August the second, 1998,' Mrs. Greyson said. 'He rolled his lorry on the M4 in thick fog. I'll never forget the phone call from the police. I had put on my guesthouse voice as you do, terrified it was Roy to say he'd be home early. But it was the police to tell me he'd been trapped inside the cab. The engine had ignited, and….'

Slim nodded. 'I can imagine.'

'At the funeral I cried in all the right places. It was easy to fake; I simply thought of the good days, and I guess I did shed a tear over the man he had once been. I was an expert at it by then. You learn how to smile in the right places when you live with a monster. And running the guesthouse … Roy was a coward. He could never look at my eyes, but there were days when my back was so bruised I could barely lift the breakfast trays.'

Slim shook away a tear. He finished the coffee and sat up. 'If there's any way I can help you—'

Mrs. Greyson gave a dry chuckle. 'I appreciate the thought, Mr. Hardy, but I'm quite all right these days. My garden doesn't take much weeding and as you've probably noticed, the guesthouse is hardly booked up flat. But if there's any time I can be of help to you … you'll find the hard stuff in the cabinet under that wobbly old clock. Don't drink it all, but if you need something to calm your nerves, no need to ask.'

'Thanks.'

'I'll add a couple of pounds on to your daily rate to cover it.' She gave an awkward wink. 'That's a joke. I don't make all that many, so perhaps it surprised you.'

Mrs. Greyson cleared up, and Slim headed up to his room. After taking a shower to wash off the previous day's soils, he pulled the clock out from under his bed and unwrapped it.

'What aren't you telling me?' he whispered, wondering if his question was addressed to the clock, or elsewhere, to the ears of someone harbouring secrets which would reveal the ultimate truth.

36

THE LITTLE VILLAGE STORE CARRIED AMPLE STOCKS to keep Slim roadworthy. With a 250ml bottle of Teachers tucked into the inner pocket of his jacket, he headed with renewed purpose to Worth Farm, the bolt cutters wrapped in a towel in his bag. With a little lubrication he had rediscovered his edge, the spark that would set the bonfire alight. He needed to get under the skin of the mystery, break the seal that was keeping him out.

The sun had dipped beneath the horizon, and the tors of Bodmin Moor were stretching long fingers across the land when he reached the top of the farm lane.

Taking the footpath through the adjacent field, he waited until he had reached the lower corner of the farmyard's grounds then climbed up into the hedge, wincing as thorns pierced his jacket, scraping the skin beneath. The climb had looked easy from the field—a bank of grass topped with a few sparse bushes through which ample gaps appeared—but the branches were lower than they looked, and the grassy bank more slippery. By the time he scrambled out the other side, his clothes were soaked and muddy, and he was bleeding from a dozen scratches.

The farmyard stood still. Late February was welcoming the warmth of March so animals were likely still out at pasture, such as there was this close to Bodmin Moor. Lights flickered in a lower window of the farmhouse on the other side of the yard, but the yard itself was silent.

He approached the shed from the side, keeping to the hedgerow, the bolt cutters slung over his shoulder. Light from the farmhouse glinted off the metal runners on the door. Slim trod through the damp grass alongside, running his fingers over the old stone walls, mind reeling with what he might find inside. When he reached the front path, he squatted low then felt for the padlock.

The chain was thinner than the padlock deserved, fitting easily into the bolt cutters' jaws. With the instrument poised, Slim paused. There was no way he could fix the chain once it was broken. He could disguise it, but the next time someone came to open the shed, they would see.

Slim pulled the bottle from his pocket and took a long swallow.

'Where are you, Amos?' he muttered, lifting the bolt cutters once more.

A growl came out of the dark, followed by a flurry of barking so close Slim felt an acute sense of panic unlike any he had felt since his days in Iraq. He froze, unable to move as something rushed at him, jaws snapping. He got the bolt cutters up just quick enough to save his face, knocking the animal aside. It went instead for his ankle, but he managed to get to his feet and stumble back as its teeth broke his skin.

An outside light came on. The farmhouse door opened and a man's voice shouted, 'Tom? What you got out there? Rat?'

Torchlight flashed across Slim's face as he struggled back towards the hedge. The man's confusion turned to outrage, a flurry of obscenities followed by something long and shiny lifting against his shoulder.

The dog let go, snarled, then came back for another try, but Slim took his chance to dive into the hedgerow. The dog, some kind of terrier, kept its distance, its feet pattering in circles as the relentless barrage of barking echoed in Slim's ears. Over the noise, Slim heard a woman shout, 'No, Trevor!', then the roar of a shotgun blast filled the air. The branches rustled, the dog squealed and fled, and a man's gruff voice shouted, 'I'll gut you if I catch you!'

As torchlight flickered in the branches above, Slim tried to slip down the other side of the fence into the field, but met a cluster of thick branches which held him in place. Instead, he wriggled deeper into the thicket, out of sight unless someone climbed up into the hedge to look.

'Did you see him?' the woman said, her voice close to the hedgerow now. Slim recognised Maggie Tinton's voice.

'He went over there. Tom took a chunk out of the bugger. Might be bleeding out.'

In a different situation, Slim would have laughed. The dog had taken a good bite of him, but a proper guard dog would have taken off half his leg.

'Did you see what he was up to?'

'Trying to get into the shed, looked like. Must have been after my bike.'

'No one would want that old thing. I don't even know why you bother with a lock.'

'If your father had—'

'Oh, quit it, Trevor. I bet it was one of those treasure hunter fools. That was Amos Birch's shed after all. I wish the blessed police would just find him and put us all to peace.'

Trevor thrust the shotgun into the hedge barely an arms' length from where Slim was crammed in between two thickets of brambles.

'I'll have a look around the perimeter, see if we can see where the sod got in. He might have dropped something. You give the police a call. Tom, come here!'

'I'm sick of this,' Maggie said. 'They just keep coming back. We get a few months of quiet and then some hooligan starts poking around, refusing to take no for an answer. I don't care how cheap it was. It wasn't worth it.'

'Don't go blaming me,' Trevor said. 'You wanted the whole lady-of-the-manor life. We had to take what we could get.'

'Well perhaps we should sell up.' They had moved away from the hedgerow now. 'I've never got used to this place. All that business with the Birch family … it leaves a sour taste.'

'Oh, stop whining and go call the police.'

'If there's no constable here within ten minutes I shall write to the council. They'll be after you for firing that gun you can be sure, but our safety—'

They rounded a building at the far side of the farmyard. The instant they were out of sight Slim was moving, squeezing through the knot of brambles, shimmying down the hedge and running through the field to the lane and his bike.

Pedaling hard, he was halfway back to the guesthouse when a police car's flickering lights appeared further down the hill. Slim jumped off the bike and crouched out of sight, holding the bike down among the weeds as the patrol car rushed past.

The guesthouse door had been latched. Panicking, Slim ran around the back, scaled the hedgerow into Mrs. Greyson's back garden, and made his way up to the back of the house. As he had hoped, she had left the back door unlocked, so he went inside, quickly pulling off his dirty clothes, which he used to wrap his even dirtier shoes.

The living room was dark and empty. He had just climbed the stairs and crept into his room when the telephone in the hall began to ring, mirrored by the muffled ringing of another phone from the room at the end of the corridor, Mrs. Greyson's room.

The ringing cut off. A door opened and footsteps trod along the landing. A knock came at the door.

'Mr. Hardy? Are you in there?'

Slim counted to ten before he answered, then muttered, 'Yes, what is it?' in the sleepiest voice he could muster.

'Oh, I'm sure it's nothing. Sorry to wake you.'

Shuffling outside. The sound of a muffled voice. Then silence.

Slim let out a breath he felt he had been holding since he fled Worth Farm. He switched on a lamp and surveyed the damage.

Brambles had left his exposed skin looking like a freshly painted latticework, but the dog bite was far worse, a line of puncture wounds that had oozed blood over his shoe.

He would have to hope the police didn't look too closely.

37

CELIA LOOKED TENSE AS SHE SMOKED HER THIRD cigarette in a row.

'I need to know,' Slim said. 'It could be important. The last person I need feeding me lies is you.'

'I didn't kill my daughter or my father,' Celia said, throwing the cigarette butt into the hedge as she leaned against the bonnet of the Ford Fiesta. The dirty grey-blue car had replaced the Metro, which she said was in for servicing.

'I'm not saying you did. There's no evidence or motive, isn't that what the police might have said? What I want to know is why you waited two days before calling the police.'

Celia's hands were shaking. Slim handed her the hip flask which she snatched out of his hand. She took a long swallow before she answered.

'My mother wanted to tidy up,' she said. 'After all, Charlotte didn't officially exist. She wanted to box away her things and hide them in one of the barns where the police wouldn't bother to look. She told me it would all come down to me, that I'd be blamed for everything. That I'd go to prison.'

With shaking hands she passed the hip flask back. Slim took a swallow before responding. Then, slowly so to be sure she understood, he said, 'See, that changes things. That's a clear attempt to pervert the course of justice. If I went to the police with this it would probably be enough to reopen the investigation, but at this point I'm still willing to give you and your mother the benefit of the doubt. Why hide Charlotte's things unless you know she's not coming back?'

Celia gave a petulant half shrug. 'The note. We knew he wasn't coming back because of the note.'

'What note?'

'He left a note. Or at least part of one.'

Slim stepped away from the car, letting the chill air of the lay-by diffuse his anger. 'A note? What the …' He clenched his fists, wrung them out. 'Is there anything else you're not telling me? Do you have it still?'

Celia shrugged. 'You have no idea how hard this is for me. I let all this go. I left it behind me. No, I don't have it, because my mother burned it on the kitchen stove, but I can remember what it said.'

Slim pulled his notebook from his pocket and held it out. 'Write it down as you remember it. Word for word. Don't miss a single word.'

Celia scowled like a scolded child but took the pad and pen and scribbled something down. 'That's it,' she said, passing it back. 'As best as I can remember.'

Slim read it aloud. "'Dear Mary, I'm sorry I have to say this to you. You have come to mean so much to me, but I'm in a bad place right now. I need some time to clear out my head, but I promise—'" He looked up at Celia. 'Why the dash?'

'Because that's where the letter ended. He didn't finish it.'

Slim sighed. 'That's it?'

Celia nodded. 'It's kind of like a suicide note, isn't it? Only he didn't finish it. He was never good with words, my father. Not like he was with his hands. "'I promise…'" I wondered for years how that sentence might have ended. "I promise to come back." "I promise never to forget you." "I promise to take good care of Charlotte." In the end, it doesn't matter, does it? He was gone, and so was she.'

'Why do you think it addressed only to your mother and not to you?'

Celia said nothing for a long time. Then, in a quiet voice, trying to hold back tears, she said, 'I wondered that for years. At the time … it broke me.'

'Broke you?'

'My mother was Hell on Earth and my personal life was a nightmare. The one constant in my life, the one thing I could depend on, was my father.'

'He took care of Charlotte? In the videos it was never you or your mother holding her. It was always your father.'

Celia coughed, bending double, her face contorting. Slim heard a reedy whistle like a motorbike's broken muffler.

'Are you all right?'

Celia looked about to scream, but there was no sound other than the haunting whistle.

'Celia?'

'She never loved me!' she wailed, loud enough to make Slim jump back. 'She belonged to him more than me. And because she didn't love me, he thought I didn't love her. And so he took her away.'

38

In the empty cafe of a 24-hour supermarket off the A30 near Bodmin, they drank laced black coffees, no longer bothering to sober up, only to stay awake until everything was said.

'I think he intended to come back,' Slim said, aware his voice was slurring. 'You've been reading it wrong. It's clear from the note what he meant.'

'Then why didn't he finish it?'

'Three reasons that could have happened,' Slim said. 'One: he changed his mind. Two: he decided not to write the note, because he intended to deliver the message in person, something he didn't do, which rules that out. And three: he was disturbed before he finished it.'

'Michael?'

Slim shrugged. 'It's possible, but you told yourself you couldn't have imagined him as a murderer. And having met him, I can't either.'

'Then who?'

'I have one theory, but it's unlikely.'

'Tell me anyway.'

'He encountered people out on the moor involved in some other kind of criminal activity, and he was killed to keep him quiet.'

Celia laughed suddenly, loud enough to make a server look up and frown. 'Are you serious? Then what happened to my daughter?'

'I don't know. Maybe she suffered the same fate. Or maybe she was sold. You read all sorts in the news these days, don't you? It's unlikely, but it happens.'

Celia scoffed. 'Rarely. Do you really believe that?'

Slim shook his head. 'No. I think there's a far simpler explanation. One that's right in front of our eyes but we're somehow missing. Is there anything else? Only the note? No more holding information back, Celia. If there's anything else you haven't told me, I need to know.'

'Nothing I recall. He left in the clothes he was wearing. He didn't even pack a bag.'

'Another reason it's likely some event stopped him coming back.' Slim reached out and touched her shoulder. 'I have to say, Celia, that at this stage I'm ninety-nine percent sure your father, and almost certainly your daughter with him, are dead.'

Celia sniffed. 'I've felt for a long time that the best I could hope to find was their bodies.'

'Here's another tack,' Slim said. Despite detesting himself for being drunk again, there was no doubt it was throwing out ideas like an out of control thresher machine. 'The buried clock I found. No one does something like that without a reason. Perhaps he went out to the moor that night to bury it, planning to come back and finish the note.'

'But what was the point of burying it at all?'

'I haven't figured that out yet.'

'And the note in the back?'

'Again, no idea.'

Celia laughed. 'You're a pretty pathetic private investigator.'

Slim shrugged. 'I was too drunk to get a real job and too lazy to kill myself.'

Midnight had come and gone. Slim wondered how far Mrs. Greyson's newfound tolerance for him would stretch.

'We need to leave,' he said.

As they were heading back to the car, Celia said, 'Thanks for helping me. I know this isn't going the way you'd like, but I appreciate it nevertheless.'

'No problem. I had nothing much going on. It's keeping my interest, that's for sure. I can't promise I'll find all of the answers, but I'll try to find some.'

They had reached the car park. Celia looked up at the sound of a distant siren.

'You know, part of me doesn't want to find out,' she said. 'I'm not sure I could handle it. It's going to be bad news, and I've had quite enough of that in my life already.'

Before he could stop himself, Slim put his hands on each of Celia's shoulders and gave them a light squeeze.

'You're still standing,' he said. 'We had a saying in

the army. If you can still get to your feet, you can still move forward. And if you can still move forward, you can still win.'

Celia smiled. For once it contained no anger or bitterness, and the years fell away. Slim saw in Celia's face the buried memory of a beautiful woman, one for whom life had soured, but one still resilient, still strong.

'You look like you're going to kiss me.'

Slim started. 'No, I—'

'You can, if you want. I mean, it's not the done thing for people of our age to get drunk and kiss in public car parks at one bloody a.m., but we could start a new trend. And it's not like I don't find you attractive. You're a little more bitter than I generally like, but I do wonder what you must have done to make your wife throw you away.'

'I guess she just spent too much time sober,' Slim said. 'I only look good in a certain light.' He started to move forward. He wanted her, he realised. He wanted this broken doll; he wanted to fix her and make her whole. Images flickered in his mind of a life together like old photographs blowing in the wind, smiles and happiness hiding a lining of pain, two people holding each other up.

He was holding her without realizing it then pulling out of a kiss he could already barely remember.

'The car's a bit small,' Celia was saying, her voice far away, 'but we could find a field somewhere. It's warm enough tonight. Not like it wouldn't be the first time…'

Slim broke away, unable to see her through the image of rough, manhandling fingers pushing her face into the earth, her mouth filling with soil that stifled a desperate cry for help. He saw her rocking back and forth then hands pushing her aside, footsteps on the road running away.

And Celia, battered, bruised and violated, forcing herself to stand, because if you could stand, you could keep moving forward. And if you could keep moving forward, you could still win.

'What's the matter?'

'Not like this.' He pushed himself away, putting a couple of parked cars between them. 'I'll call you, Celia. I'll call you when we're both feeling better.'

'Slim!' Her eyes flared with a sudden rage, flame-filled, her face contorted with more than just anger, with hate.

'Don't walk away from me!'

'I'll call you,' he shouted, breaking into a run as the distant siren blared again like a subconscious warning, not sure if he ever would but afraid not to, aware that he had to choose whether he burned with Celia or drowned without her, while all the time, the only thing he could see was the smiling face of an old man, gently patting the back of a child held in his arms.

39

HE HITCHED A LIFT UP THE A30 IN THE CAB OF A friendly but garrulous truck driver who insisted on recanting a forgettable life story which made the journey up to the Penleven turning feel far longer than it perhaps was. His anger replaced by regret, Slim leaned against the window, nodding or responding when necessary, until the truck pulled off at a roundabout and the driver bid him a safe journey home.

Determined to avoid such situations again, Slim tossed the bottle and its remaining contents into the hedge just outside the village, at the end of an hour-long downhill march, but, hitting his bed at pence after two, he marveled at a world that had got him home from the butt end of nowhere at a reasonable time, with at least part of his sanity intact.

His luck was looking up.

Mrs. Greyson was reticent at breakfast, as though she had slept through Slim's latest indiscretions. The thumping hangover meant everything tasted of potential vomit and it wasn't until a few hours later, and following a walk around the village ostensibly to clear his head, but in reality an attempt to recall where he had thrown his leftover whisky, that he began to feel better.

No longer relying on Mrs. Greyson's honesty, the village store's post office cubicle was holding a package for him. Slim took it to a bench on the small patch of parkland that served as Penleven's village green and opened it up. Kay had returned the video tape, along with a folder of notes. Hands steadied by a single swig of a whisky miniature flicked through the enclosed documents. Along with a handwritten note were several computer printouts.

He looked at each as he consulted Kay's notes.

"'I passed your tape to a friend in forensics,'" Slim read, saying the words out loud as though that would help them to stick. "'The quality is remarkably poor, even for the mid-nineties. Something very bottom range, but the cameraman needs a little help working a focus. I couldn't get everything you wanted, but I got some. The logo on the picture over the desk is the British Clockmaker's Guild.'"

Slim lifted the printout of an enlarged version of the logo, with a grainy screenshot in the corner showing the original.

'And I picked a stamp off that single table shot about fourteen minutes in. Germany. Specifically it's a picture of Frankfurt Cathedral. Something commemorative? I'd guess you could get a time estimate if you figured that one out. Stamps like that are collector's items; they're rarely used for actual mail. And the logo on the side of the box belongs to a horticulturalist company in the Black Forest. You owe me big for that one. My guy got me the name but it took me a couple of days to track that one down. I've enclosed a phone number.'

Slim flicked over a few more pages, nodding slowly. A German horticulturalist. A wood supplier. Slim's research had told him that cuckoo clocks had been invented in the Black Forest region of southern Germany. Was it possible Amos Birch had made a pilgrimage to what he might have considered a spiritual home?

Slim had dialed the number before remembering there was no reception down here in Penleven. He took a deep breath. He was getting ahead of himself.

'"The shoes by the door are a pair of Clark's,"' Kay's notes continued as Slim read. '"Hiking boots, but they make good farm boots too. I've enclosed a photo of a tread but it might not be exactly the right type. Check with the manufacturer. And the jacket, my contact couldn't figure it out, but it's possibly a no-name brand. Supermarket type. That's all I've got, but like I say, you owe me! P.S. damn, that was one creepy video."'

Slim frowned, wondering what Kay meant. The video had unsettled him too, but only because it showed two missing people, probably dead.

He put the package and its contents into his backpack and headed back through the village. He spotted Michael ploughing a field and waited by the gate until the farmhand noticed him.

Michael continued to work for a few minutes before turning the tractor around and driving over.

'I've told you everything,' he said by way of greeting.

Slim shook his head. 'I'm not the police, Michael. Nothing you say is official.'

'You could be bugged.'

Slim laughed. 'Do I look that efficient? I guess I could be, but you'll have to trust me that I'm not. Look, for what it's worth, I don't think you killed anyone. I don't think you've done anything wrong, in fact. However, I do think you saw something that night, and I want you to tell me what it was.'

Michael looked everywhere but at Slim. He wrung his hands together, shaking his head.

'I didn't kill anyone,' he said again.

'You saw him, didn't you?'

'Who?'

'Quit the games, Michael. I have places to go and you have work to do. You know who I mean.'

Michael grimaced. He ran a hand through his hair then turned around as though looking for support from someone hitherto unseen. With a sigh, he turned back to Slim and nodded.

'I was hiding down in the trees by the river. I heard shouting, so I came up to the yard to see what was going on. I heard a door slam. Someone came out, walking fast. They went into that little outhouse, the one he used for a workshop. He was in there a few minutes then he came out. Had a bag over his shoulder and something in his arms.'

'Did you see what?'

Michael shook his head. 'Could have been anything. It was wrapped up in a towel, a thick blanket maybe.'

'Was it moving at all?'

'Moving? No. But he was holding it with both arms as though it was really important.'

Slim nodded. The bundle had to be Charlotte. But was she sleeping, drugged, or even dead when Amos carried her away?

'Now, this is vital, Michael. There used to be two ways out of the yard, didn't there? The vehicle lane, and a path down through where that hedge is now. I saw that stone wall down there. Your handiwork, wasn't it? You built it for the Tintons, didn't you?'

Michael nodded. 'Maggie Tinton called me up a year after they bought the place. She didn't like that people could get in from two directions, even though technically it's blocking a public right-of-way.' He smiled. 'It's not officially there.'

Slim rolled his eyes. 'Pot calling the kettle black,' he muttered.

'What?'

'Nothing. I had a run in with her, that's all.'

Michael shrugged. 'She's spiky, but she's got nothing on old Mary. How did you know when I built that?'

'It protrudes a little from the rest of the hedgerow to allow for the spread of those trees' roots. It was clearly built after they were planted, possibly a few years later, because any closer and the lower branches would have got in your face while you worked, meaning you would have cut them back or likely broken a couple, yet the lower boughs showed no signs of damage.'

'Aren't you quite the detective?' Michael muttered.

'They found boot prints in the mud heading that way,' Slim continued, quietly pleased at the grudging note of respect in Michael's voice. 'The boot prints matched a pair of boots Amos owned. But there was a concrete path down to the edge of the property. I've seen it in … photos. For a keen moors walker like Amos, he'd have known where that path was with his eyes closed and he wouldn't have risked slipping in the mud, not if he was carrying something valuable. They were your prints, weren't they?'

Michael sighed. 'Damn, you're good, I'll give you that. We had the same brand. Common work men's boots. Not a lot of shoe shops in Camelford.'

'You slipped when you were running away. You must have known you left prints. What happened to your boots?'

'I threw them in a skip outside Bodmin a couple of days later while I was out buying fencing supplies. After I heard the police got called in. The police asked to see my work boots so I showed them a different pair I sometimes used out on the tractor. They get really muddied up when the fields are waterlogged—'

Slim lifted a hand. 'So let me get this straight. The boot prints that were the main evidence to suggest Amos Birch headed out onto the moors were not made by Amos, but by you.'

Michael sighed again. 'Right.'

'And you bolted because you saw him come out of his workshop?'

'Yeah, I saw him go off with that gear, and I thought

I'd better get out of there. Something just felt weird, you know? Like I was seeing something I shouldn't have seen.'

'I have one last question then I'll leave you in peace. Which way did he go?'

'Up the lane towards the main road.'

Slim nodded. Another piece had fallen into place. 'And you're being truthful with me, aren't you?'

Michael put a hand over his chest. 'I swear that's everything. I didn't kill anyone. I might not have said everything when the police came round, but I was scared. And what does it matter whether he went onto the moor or up to the road?'

'I don't know if it matters at all,' Slim said. 'Thanks, Michael. You've helped a lot.'

He left the farmhand to his business. So, Amos hadn't gone onto the moor at all. It removed many of the possibilities running through Slim's mind, but it also added a few more.

Wherever Amos had gone, he had gone there with purpose, but something had happened to prevent him ever coming back.

40

IT TOOK SLIM THREE PHONE CALLS TO DISCOVER THAT Amos Birch's membership to the British Clockmaking Guild had been rejected just three months before his disappearance. A longstanding clerk sounded almost proud to tell him that Amos had rejected the society's rules of membership, which governed the production of clocks and watches, and his scheduled attendance at a prestigious clockmaker's fair had been cancelled.

From his vantage point on a hill looking out at Bodmin Moor, Slim began calling clockmakers in the Black Forest. Some spoke no English, others knew Amos Birch by reputation but not personally. Slim's phone was nearly out of battery when he remembered the number Kay had given him.

A gruff voice answered in German. Slim introduced himself and discovered that the man—a wood supplier and clock dealer called Ralph Schwimmer—spoke decent English. Slim explained who he was and told

Schwimmer he was on the trail of the missing Amos Birch.

'My father retired in 1998,' Schwimmer explained. 'He might have known Herr Birch.'

'Would it be possible to speak to your father?'

'I'm afraid not. He died last year. If it's helpful, I could have a look through his old correspondence for anything relating to Amos Birch. I have heard the name.'

'Thanks. I'd really appreciate it.'

Slim hiked back down to Penleven and headed to the Crown for dinner. On a chilly Thursday night June was alone in the bar. Slim ordered a beer to wash down a plate of chips, then felt a sudden hardening of his resolve and refused to drink it, letting it sit while he stared at it like an artifice of the devil himself.

'It's been a few days since I last saw you,' June said. 'Have you solved the big mystery yet?'

Slim shrugged. 'I've only created more questions. I don't suppose you know who frequented this place in the early nineties?'

'I could find out. What is it you're specifically after?'

'I want a list of staff and regulars circa 1993.'

June laughed. 'You don't ask for much, do you?'

'I'm looking for someone who might have committed a crime.'

'What kind of crime?'

'A rape.'

June's eyes widened. 'What does that have to do with Amos Birch?'

'I'm not sure yet.'

'Well, you could start with that lot above the bar.'

Slim looked up. 'Where?'

'There. The picture of the darts team in 1993. They won the cup that year. If you want a conclusive list of regulars, you don't need to look much further than that. We're not overrun with participants round here. Anything like that is pretty much all hands on deck.'

June came around the bar, reached up and unhooked a dusty, faded photograph from above the bar. She took a cloth and wiped it down, then laid it out in front of him.

Seven men stood in a line, with the man in the middle holding up a trophy. Another bigger man stood slightly off to the side, while in the background, Slim recognized the Crown's bar.

'That one there's old Reg,' June said, indicating a middle-aged version of the old-timer who propped up the bar. 'Those two youngsters are Michael and Davy.'

Davy, Slim remembered, was Michael's skinny drinking buddy. But while Davy had a bored look on his face, a cherubic Michael beamed at the camera.

'Handsome lad,' Slim said. 'Amazing what time can do.'

June laughed. 'Ah, he's still doing okay. Believe it or not, I used to look okay with the lights on too.'

Slim let his laughter give her the benefit of the doubt.

'Any of these other guys still around?'

'That one, that's Les. Doesn't come in much these days. Grew out of pub life, maybe, although you see him pottering around his garden now he's retired. That one's old Bob—he's long gone, by all accounts. That's Ted, used to work in the China clay quarry, lost him to cancer just a couple of years back. The big guy's Alan, the old landlord … and that guy with the beard, I'm not sure who that is, but he doesn't come in anymore.'

Slim stared at the last face, feeling a hint of recognition.

'I don't suppose you'd have a list of fixtures for that year, would you?'

June lifted an eyebrow. 'Slim, this is pub darts, not the Premiership. I doubt if there ever was a list of fixtures. Then, as now, I expect, games were on a Wednesday. One week at home, the next away. The league runs from Oct right through the end of March.'

'On a Wednesday. Thanks.'

'Are you going to drink that beer? Or do you want me to pour you a cold one? I'm enjoying the company but I prefer not to drink alone.'

The door rattled and old Reg marched in. He missed a step as he took in Slim, then recovered himself to reach his regular stool.

'Actually,' Slim said, 'I'll have one for me and whatever Reg is drinking.'

'Don't mind if I do,' Reg muttered as June gave Slim a sly wink. Then, noticing the picture, Reg said, 'What's all this then?'

Before Slim could speak, June said, 'Slim here's thinking of buying a property in the area. Wanted to get to know a few locals.'

'Oh aye.'

'You've aged well, Reg.'

The old man coughed. 'Sense of humour like that and you'll fit right in.'

'June was just showing me some old pictures. I recognise a couple of guys, eh. I met Les the other day, and that's Michael—'

Reg shook his head. Slim had deliberately indicated the man with the beard, but Reg pointed to the real picture of Michael.

'No, that's Michael there. That guy with the beard … god, I forget his name. John, maybe. He was one of Davy's college friends at Mahjons in Plymouth. Didn't used to drink here, but was a deadeye and we were short. He didn't come back the next season and we finished fifth.'

'What happened to him?'

'Graduated college, got a job, I'd guess. Davy didn't come back either—got a job in the shipyards for a few years until his ma died. He wasn't much of a loss though —we used to try and fix the draw so he took one of their certain winners.'

They both laughed and clinked glasses. Slim reluctantly took a sip.

'For an out-of-towner, you're all right, lad.'

'Thanks.'

'Still on the trail of old Amos?'

'I'm still interested, but I'm close to giving it up. There's nothing to go on.'

'He was after a list of regulars from ninety-three,' June said. 'Something about a rape.'

Slim shot June a sharp look but it was too late. Reg turned to Slim, eyes hardening.

'What does anything like that have to do with Amos Birch? Weren't no rape around then that I remember. You want to be careful what you go around saying about people.'

'I haven't accused anyone of anything, and I'm not about to.'

'Who is it who's supposed to have been raped?'

Slim took a deep breath, wondering if he was about to kick the hornet's nest one time too many.

'Celia Birch. I heard something, is all.'

Reg coughed a mouthful of beer across the bar. June frowned as she reached for a cloth.

'What I heard about that girl was you'd only need to slip her a fiver and she was yours for the night. Weren't no need to get yourself involved in some criminal rubbish.'

'Reg, you shouldn't talk like that,' June said.

'Just me opinion,' Reg said. 'Nothing wrong with that, is there? If you ask me, people pussyfoot too much around what they really mean.'

'We're not asking you, Reg,' June said. Banished, Reg grumbled inaudibly into his pint while June turned to Slim. 'What did you hear?'

'That Celia might have been the victim of an assault, and that the person responsible might have been involved in Amos Birch's disappearance.'

It wasn't an outright lie, but Slim figured he might as well add his own speculation to the mix. He wondered if, among the jousting of rumour, hearsay, and lies, one story would arise victorious.

'Never heard nothing about it,' Reg grumbled, not looking up.

'Was there ever a rumour that Celia Birch might have had a child?' Slim asked. 'I mean, she worked here, didn't she? It would have been obvious, I'd have thought.'

Reg shook his head. I never heard a thing. Although the girl did pull a vanishing act. It's been so long that I can't put timeframes on these things, but she worked down the kitchen a few nights a week, then she stopped and Alan got someone else in.'

'Can you remember what time of year, even?'

Reg shrugged. 'Spring, maybe? Just as business was picking up. Left Alan in the lurch, I'll say. I remember Mike and Davy down in that kitchen for a few nights. Alan paid them in beer, as I recall, even though the lads were underage.'

Reg chuckled as though that was his best memory of the year.

'Girl was fifteen, wasn't she?' June said.

'About that.'

'Probably quit to go swot for her exams.'

Slim looked from one to the other. Reg frowned, then shrugged. June smiled.

'You boys might like your stories, but you can't find a mystery in everything.'

Slim remembered school well enough to recall that few kids spent much time swotting for their fifth-year exams. It wasn't an impossible scenario, but Celia hadn't come across to Slim as a particularly studious person. He had been considering that the whole rape tale might have been a cover up for something salubrious to which she didn't want to admit—an affair with a well-known married man, for example.

'Where you been hearing these things, anyway?' Reg asked.

Slim shrugged. 'Around.'

'Place like this, there ain't much else to do but throw around talk. Now, if old Amos showed up again, that'd be something, wouldn't it?'

'What do you remember about his wife?'

Reg lifted an eyebrow. 'Think she knocked him off, do you?'

Slim shook his head. 'Far as I can see she had no motive. She was wheelchair-bound and sick. Couldn't work. No income but disability apart from what he brought in.'

'That's about what I remember,' Reg said. 'The Birches—save that daughter of theirs—didn't get out much. He was a recluse by design, she by circumstance. Used to see him out in the fields from time to time, and he'd go around to fix a clock if you asked him, but he wasn't exactly Mr. Parish Council.'

'So you didn't know her well?'

'He met her up country, I remember,' Reg said. 'At one of his clock functions. He then took over his old man's farm, and she had no choice but to come down here with him. She never really took to country life. You'd hear her in the store from time to time, snapping that they didn't have this type of cereal, or that type of bread. No one much liked her, but she didn't seem to care. Then she starts getting sick. You'd not see her for months, then it would be with a stick, then a walker, then a chair. By all accounts she was bed-bound by the time the end came.'

'And Celia looked after her?'

'God, no. That girl was gone almost as soon as he was. Might have popped in from time to time, but there was always a home help outside, parked in their yard.'

'Where did Celia go?'

'Washed her hands of it. Girl always was bigger than Penleven, if you get my meaning. And had probably run out of men to snare.'

'Reg!'

The old man lifted a hand. 'Sorry love, just I never liked her, eh. Girl didn't fit in round here.'

Without realizing it, Slim had drunk his way through three pints. The old clock above the bar showed just after ten, but it was that point of the night where Slim had to make a decision. He could try to leave now, or he could wake up in a ditch somewhere, covered in his own vomit.

He pushed himself to his feet, alarmed at how unsteady he felt.

'Thanks for the conversation,' he said. 'I'd better turn in. Ghosts to hunt tomorrow.'

'Good luck, boy,' Reg said.

After June too wished him goodnight, Slim stumbled out into the dark. Halfway back to the guesthouse, he felt an overwhelming need to call Celia, partly to apologise for rejecting her, and partly to keep her up-to-date on what he had discovered.

He continued walking, up past the guesthouse and

along the road that gradually rose out of Penleven's valley towards the A39 to Camelford. As soon as the mast indicator on his phone appeared, he dialed Celia's number.

It was late, and she was likely working, so he didn't expect an answer. Words were tumbling over themselves to be left in a cluttered, jumbled order on her voicemail, but the dialing tone never came. Slim tried again, then a third time.

Staring at the display which even in his intoxicated state he could see clearly said *Celia Mobile*, he frowned.

Her phone was either switched off or had got broken somehow, which, given the circumstances, was unexpected.

41

THE NEXT MORNING, WITH A THUMPING HEADACHE HE had come to expect, he tried calling Celia's number again, but got the same lack of dial tone. He checked the number to the one he had written down, and found no mistake. Celia had gone offline.

Unable to contact her, he instead turned his attention to some of his new leads. He caught a local bus into Camelford and walked up a steep hill to a quiet public library, where he found out that Marjohns was a euphemism for The College of St. Mark and St. John, a possible explanation for the nickname of the man Reg remembered only as John. When he called their administrative office, however, he was told that in order for them to track down a former student, he'd need more information than a nickname of John and a prowess at darts.

Stumped for the time being, he moved onto his next lead. Something Maggie Tinton had said to her husband in the yard at Worth Farm had got caught in Slim's mind and now rattled around like a marble in a glass jar.

She had referred to the farm as cheap. Glancing through a copy of the local newspaper, Slim found no farms for sale with a price even close to cheap, several in the seven-figure region. Using the newspaper as a guide, he rang around the local estate agents, trying to find out who had listed the sale. When that line of enquiry came up blank, he called up a couple of local property auctioneers on a whim, and finally found it.

The property had gone to auction in late 2006, six months after Mary Birch's death. However, it hadn't been listed by Celia Birch, but by the bank.

Worth Farm had been sold as a repossession.

As a family farm, Slim found it hard to believe that the Birches had still been paying a mortgage, and surely any debts could have been cleared with the sale of an outlying field or two.

Getting hold of the auction house responsible, he discovered that Worth Farm had been remortgaged in the mid-nineties, and payments had been rare or late thereafter. By the time of Mary Birch's death, the family had been virtually bankrupt.

Where had the Birch family wealth gone? Celia might have the answer, but her phone was still disconnected.

He was beginning to worry about her safety. She had said she worked as a nurse, so Slim found the numbers for all the major hospitals in Plymouth and rang to enquire. By the time he finished his last call half an hour later, his worry had turned to suspicion. None had either a Celia Birch or a Celia Merrifield on their staff roster.

It was too late to check on her, because by the time he had walked back to the bus stop, he had missed the last bus to Tavistock. Instead, he headed back to Penleven. Just off the A39 he got off early so he could check his phone for messages as he walked down the hill.

It was nearly half past five and he found even Penleven had a semblance of a rush hour, with an emphasis on the rush. Several times he dived into the hedge to avoid being mowed down by returning commuters far more confident on the roads than he would be. As he reached the crossroads just above the village where connecting lanes headed right to Trelee or left to another village called Culminster, a dirty Escort hacked past him, cut left, and accelerated down the hill. Slim considered an irate wave, but he recognised the man at the wheel. He turned down the lane, hearing the car engine cut out just over the brow of the next hill.

Five minutes later, he arrived at a row of three tatty council houses. The Escort was parked outside the middle one, and as Slim reached the gate he saw Davy coming out of a garage, holding a wrench. Davy hadn't seen Slim, so Slim watched as the scrawny man opened the car's bonnet and began poking around inside.

After a couple of minutes, Davy swore, then slammed the bonnet back down. He tossed the wrench in the direction of the garage and made for the front door.

'Hey, Davy.'

Davy turned. A cigarette poised in his fingers fell to the ground.

'What the hell do you want?'

Slim leaned against the car and pulled out a coffee flask he had bought in Camelford. It was filled with water, but he hoped the casualness would disarm Davy, who looked tense enough to snap.

'Nice place you've got here. Needs a new coat of paint, but you've got a decent view, especially if you took a chainsaw to that second tree over there. How was work?'

Davy took a couple of steps closer. 'I said, what do you want?'

'I was just passing.'

'On your way to where? Only thing up that way is an abattoir.'

'I was in the mood for steak. I like it fresh, still twitching if at all possible.'

'You're leaning on my car.'

'I know. I'm getting grime on my coat.'

'Mike said you were a nosy bastard. I was wondering when my turn would come. This it, is it?'

'I only want to talk. It's about Celia Birch.'

'What about her?'

Break it open. Stamp it if you have to. Open it up to see what's inside.

'You're what, fifty years old?'

'What's it to you?'

'And you're living in a council house.'

'Better than living in a guesthouse.'

Touché. Slim hid a smile. 'You've been a regular of the Crown most of your life, haven't you?'

'So? Nothing else to do round here. What's that got to do with Celia?'

'Was she a girlfriend of yours, back when she used to wash up in the Crown?'

'What are you talking about? She was just a kid.'

'A pretty one. Popular, so I've heard.'

'Are you calling me a pervert?'

Slim took a step closer, deliberately putting himself in range if Davy fancied a swing. *Temptation is the key to a confession*, he remembered an old negotiator friend telling him. Draw them out. Deceive them. Let them think they can win.

'Celia used to walk home alone, all the way up to Worth Farm. Wasn't there a time when you might have seen her, found yourself tempted? Everyone knew her reputation. No one would have believed her over you.'

'I'm not like that. You're crazy.'

'I have it on good authority that Celia was attacked one night on her way home. It was a Wednesday. Darts night. You played darts, didn't you, Davy?'

'I never did nothing to anyone!'

Slim leaned back against the car again. He took another sip of coffee.

'Then who else could it have been?'

Davy gave a frantic shake of his head. 'Don't know.'

'Come on, Davy, you can do better than that. Give me an idea. If you don't I'll have no choice but to think you're lying.' Slim took a step forward, puffing out his chest. 'I'm ex-army. I've seen a lot of bad things. And one thing always upset me more than anything else: the abuse of minors. You know what I'm talking about, don't you? She was underage, Davy. That makes you a—'

'It wasn't me!'

'Give me a name. I don't care how unlikely you think it might be. Just a name. I'll find out the rest.'

Davy gave a violent shake of his head as though searching through his thoughts like a magic eight ball, looking for an answer. He frowned, then jutted his head forward, and finally let out a little cough. 'I bet it was him,' he said, looking up at Slim. 'He always used to perv over her, said he could have her any time.'

'Who?'

'Johnny.'

'Who's Johnny?'

'Me mate from Marjons. Didn't work out for me up there. Just took a bit of free money, got drunk, laid a few times. After I came back, we needed a sub for the team. I remembered Johnny, called him up. He wouldn't play home games, just in case she saw him. Didn't even want to come in for the team pic, after we won. She was gone by then, though. Left Alan in the shit.'

'Why wouldn't he come in?'

'In case she saw him, shopped him in.'

'To who?'

'His class.'

Slim felt a hot flush run down his back. 'His class? What class? What were you studying up at Marjons?'

'Teacher training. Like I say, I didn't cut it. Johnny, though, he ended up doing geography, something like that. Don't see him now. Nothing to talk about, what with him being a posh teacher and me working up the pasty factory.'

'How did Johnny get home after darts matches?'

'Drive, I guess. We'd get dropped off at the Crown. I'd stay for a pint but he'd get straight off back to Plymouth.'

'Can you get to Plymouth by taking the Trelee road?'

'Yeah, course. It comes out on the A30. Just go straight across.'

'Do you remember Johnny's second name?'

'Oh, Johnny wasn't his real name. We just called him that, posh twat. Marjons and all. Guy was full of himself. Thought he was Phil Taylor.'

Slim felt that tickling flush again.

'What was Johnny's real name?'

'Nick. Nick Jones.'

42

'SO, DO YOU KNOW WHEN FILMING WILL START?' NICK asked, sipping the latte he had ordered from the bar. Slim had ordered a pint, and was struggling with the urge to smash it, glass and all, into Nick's face.

You have no proof, he reminded himself. *Even with the coincidence, it's all just a hunch unless you get a confession.* Out loud, he said, 'By the end of the month. I just wanted to meet you in person again to let you know that your interview will be a pivotal part.'

Nick grinned. 'That sounds grand.'

'I just need to clarify some information.'

'Sure, shoot away.'

'You were Celia Birch's homeroom teacher in Liskeard Secondary during her GCSE exam year in 1993?'

Nick nodded. Slim noticed him looking over Slim's shoulder, as though something outside the window were more interesting.

'Yeah, that's right.'

'I just wanted to be certain, so I did a little background check—just to make sure our facts are accurate, you understand—and according to records currently held by your school you would have been a student teacher on placement at that time.'

Nick's eyes met Slim's for the first time. 'Ah, well, it's a long time ago now. I might have got a couple of details mixed up. I was just supposed to be observing, you know, but the lazy bastard supposed to be mentoring me treated me like his little admin bunny, dumping all his work on me so I was practically doing his job for him.'

'You see, I remember you had a few things to say about Celia. I wondered how a teacher might hear such playground talk, but if you were assisting the class's main teacher, you might have been closer to the kids than most teachers usually get.'

Nick scratched his ear. His gaze returned to the window.

'And you would have been what, twenty-two? I mean, there's that obvious age gap, but far less than most teachers, am I right?'

'Yeah, I guess. How much digging did you do?' Nick gave a nervous laugh. 'You get goss on my drinking habits too?'

Slim leaned forward. 'As it happens … I told you, Nick, that I'm a researcher. I research. I heard another rumour about Celia. That she dropped out because she got assaulted. Raped. You never heard that?'

Nick shook his head. 'No, didn't hear that.'

Slim stood up and wandered over to a pool table. He

brushed the surface with the back of his hand, then pulled out his wallet.

'You play?'

Nick shook his head. 'Not much.'

'Don't have a fifty coin anyway.' Slim turned to a dartboard nearby. 'Throw? I'm pretty useless but I can hit the board.'

Nick shrugged. 'Not really. Might have played once or twice.'

Slim frowned. 'Really? I heard somewhere you played for the Crown down in Penleven.'

Nick shrugged. 'I might have helped them out a couple of times.'

'Must have been awkward, what with Celia working down in the kitchens.'

Nick scratched his other ear. 'I never saw her. Like I say, it was only once or twice.'

Slim sighed. 'A shame. I hoped you might have been able to offer up some insights on the regulars down there. I'm pretty convinced one of them might have been responsible.'

Nick nodded. In the glare of the pool table's light a sheen of sweat was visible on his brow.

'I mean, there's no chance they could prosecute someone now. It's far too gone for that. Not unless Celia really did have a kid as a result, but there's no evidence to suggest that. Only those rumours you told me.' As Nick stared off into space, Slim laughed. 'She was probably asking for it, though. A slut like her. Wasn't she, Nick?'

'I'd better go,' Nick said.

Slim grinned and slapped Nick on the shoulder, noticing how the other man flinched.

'Call me, Nick, if you remember anything else?'

'Sure.'

Slim watched Nick stumble out, a shadow of the cocky, aloof man who had walked in less than an hour before. Slim slammed a fist into his palm. He wanted to go after Nick, drag him into an alley somewhere, then punch and punch and punch until Nick had no face left to wear his smug grins, but it would serve no greater purpose.

He finished his beer then went outside to make a call to another old friend from the Armed Forces.

'Slim Hardy? That you?' came a familiar voice. 'It's been a while, buddy. You're still on that old number then?'

'I don't move well with the times, Don. I'm like a ship stuck in ice. I know it's been a while, but I need to ask a favour.'

Donald Lane had toured Iraq with Slim in the early nineties. Whereas Slim had derailed his own career, Don had left on his terms, later forming an intelligence consultancy that often worked directly with the government.

'Shoot, Slim. I've got your back. Like in the old days, right?'

Slim held up the smartphone Nick had left behind. In his haste to leave, the teacher had failed to notice Slim slip it off their table and put it on a stool where it would be easy to deny any involvement had Nick seen. He turned it over in his hand.

'I need to crack a phone code,' he said. He told Don the brand, and the other laughed.

'Easy. Yours?'

'An acquaintance. Then I need you to dig some dirt. Enough to ruin a career.'

43

SLIM STARED UP AT CELIA'S WINDOW WHILE THE RAIN pattered around him. The curtains were drawn, no lights on, no sign of either car he had known her to drive.

She hadn't answered when he rang the bell, neither when he tried the phone. A couple of neighbours he had spoken to claimed not to have contact with her, that she was secretive, kept herself to herself. It wasn't a surprise to Slim, who had never made any attempt to associate with his own neighbours in times past, and rarely they with him.

It did nothing to allay his fears, though, and his concern for Celia's welfare was growing.

For the first time, he entertained the possibility that his digging might have stirred up too many bees, that someone dangerous was no longer dormant and was stalking the streets.

He headed for the town library where he

photocopied a list of all public and private medical establishments in the Cornwall and Devon central area. Celia had said she worked as a nurse, but perhaps she hadn't meant in the conventional sense. There were a dozen possibilities—care homes, dentistry, even school nursing. Slim found a café near the bus station and started calling through the list, asking if a Celia Birch or Merrifield was on the roster.

By the time the last bus back to Penleven was pulling in, he was only down as far as G, and had so far drawn a blank. He was tired, his ear aching from the hard press of his phone, and his battery was almost gone.

He was heading for the bus when he felt a buzz in his pocket.

The number wasn't one he recognised from the last couple of hours of conversations. Slim stepped out of the queue to answer.

'Herr Hardy?' came an unfamiliar voice. 'This is Ralph Schwimmer. We spoke the other day?'

Slim was so excited he could barely respond.

'I called to tell you I found a couple of boxes of my father's old letters. There was some correspondence with Herr Birch. I can fax copies to you if that would please you.'

Slim wanted to fist-pump the air. 'I'd be most grateful, thank you. I'll call you back with a fax number tomorrow. Can you tell me briefly if there was anything related to Mr. Birch's disappearance?'

'Nothing like that,' Ralph said. 'But there was correspondence relating to a visit in spring of 1996. Herr Birch was quite insistent that he would be arriving in early March, intending to stay a few months with my father. From his letters I gathered that they planned to share techniques and perhaps collaborate on a few projects.'

Slim's hands were shaking. By the bus door, the driver was calling for any last passengers.

'So he was planning to go to the Black Forest?'

'Yes. However, I talked to my mother, who is in a care home. Her memory isn't good now, but she told me she never recalled Herr Birch ever visiting.'

'Thank you so much. I'll be in touch with that fax number.'

As Slim hung up and ran past the driver's irate glare onto the bus, his mind reeled.

He had Amos Birch's intended destination. Perhaps struggling with his family life or just needing a break, he had planned to visit a friend.

So what had happened to stop him ever getting there?

44

THE FAXED LETTERS WERE WAITING AT THE POST office the next morning. Slim bought a celebratory can of beer and retired to the village green's bench to read through them.

Although outwardly a quiet man, Amos had a lot to say in the written form. A lot of it was largely over Slim's head: technical information relating to the construction of clocks, carving methods, mechanical terminology. Occasionally Amos would insert little snippets of his personality: '*...I've found it harder to concentrate of late...*', '*...I sometimes wonder if there is a futility in hunting perfection of the mind when one's life is calamitous...*', '*...my workshop has always been my solace, where I can shut out the traumas of the outside world...*'.

It wasn't until later letters planning the visit that Amos really began to reveal himself.

'I am yet to inform those closest to me of my intention to leave for a while. It is likely to cause some distress, both within my

household and without, but my life has become a spring so tightly wound that I fear leaving it untended any longer. You understand, my dear friend, that we all need to escape sometime, but those that truly care will withhold their judgement and wait until one's return, however long that may be.'

Slim nodded. He took out a pen and underlined a few key expressions.

My household and without.

Escape.

However long.

Later letters went into further detail, and Slim found the first solid mention of family.

'My daughter concerns me greatest, for her state of mind continues to worsen. Her mother is little help, badgering the girl relentlessly. I have done what I can to ease her trauma, but Charlotte's presence helps less and less, it seems. It was only ever my intention to ever bring my daughter peace, but I fear the trauma of her mother's actions and the supposed lesson-learning she has repeatedly espoused to excuse her cruelty. However, despite my distaste, she is also a woman not of her right mind, and for that, some excuses can be made. Her illness has destroyed her, but I feel it is my fault. Perhaps if I had never brought her here....'

Slim shook his head. Amos came across as an extremely articulate man caught in a web of misfortune.

The last letter, though, was the most revealing of all.

'I have made my plans. We will travel overland, as I have never been fond of flying and you miss so much, don't you think? I have booked us tickets on the ferry from Plymouth to Santander, from where I fancy we might travel by train. I fear the repercussions my absence might have, but I have already arranged additional help around the farm and the house. My wife will

understand, and if not, maybe that will be telling. It will be good for Celia too, to get away from Worth Farm for a while, to see a bit of Europe. That might make a difference. I can but hope. I will first ensure both Charlotte and my current unfinished project are safe from any wrathful repercussions, then I hope I and my daughter will be with you, my good friend, in the day or two following the fourth.'

'Huh.' Slim shook his head. It was there, in black and white: Amos had planned to take an extended overseas trip. He hadn't walked away from his family, and had even planned to take Celia with him.

So little still made sense, but another piece of the jigsaw had fallen into place. Amos had never intended to disappear, so something must have befallen him.

Who were the suspects? Was Michael lying again? Could Nick have worse in him than rape?

Slim shook his head. He had already ruled out Michael. Nick was a monster for sure, but Slim couldn't see the school teacher as a murderer. Intuition was a strange thing. Slim had been often wrong, but Nick was the kind of guy who preyed on young women, not men in their prime. He was a pathetic coward, but no killer.

Someone else, then?

Slim squeezed his temples. He was missing something vital. He knew it.

45

THE NEXT DAY WAS SATURDAY, MEANING NO BUSES RAN to Tavistock. He walked up the village to his regular vantage point and called Celia, but again received no answer.

His concern was boiling over to outright worry. He'd turned down—regrettably, now he considered it—a pass, but no woman he'd ever known would have stayed angry so long. Not when he was also technically in her employ.

There was so much he needed to tell her. The letters, his suspicion of Nick Jones, the evidence linking the teacher to the Penleven area. Then there were the letters: proof that Amos hadn't forgotten his daughter, that he had even intended to take her with him.

There was so much he needed to ask too. Where had the family money gone? Who might Amos have trusted enough to leave Charlotte and his current project with while he went overseas?

And while it might hurt to unearth memories perhaps long buried, he wanted to know more about Celia's supposed state of mind, and her mother's alleged cruelty.

A clue could come from anywhere.

After exhausting his phone's battery on the next twenty health-related establishments in his list—half of which were closed due to the weekend—he headed back to the guesthouse.

March had come on without him realising, and before he could make it up the stairs, Mrs. Greyson accosted him to help bring some garden furniture out of the shed.

She rewarded him with another special coffee on the back veranda, but this time her conversation barely strayed from the casual: observations about general village life, her garden, the moor. Slim found their talk so relaxing that he was almost sad when she stood up to clear the tea things away.

Up in his room, Slim pulled the clock out from under his bed and ran his fingers over the carvings as he listened to the gentle ticking.

Unfinished. Amos had carried it off to hide it somewhere safe, but had never returned.

Slim had put Kay's copy of the note in the same bag and now pulled it out too. Amos had carried Charlotte off with him, but something had happened to the little girl.

Charlotte.

I will first ensure both Charlotte and my current unfinished project are safe…

A clock, as Slim had found, could be buried. But what had Amos Birch intended for the little girl? Where had he taken her?

Over the weeks Slim had built up quite a picture of Amos, Mary and Celia, but Charlotte remained a mystery. He knew nearly nothing about her other than what he had seen on the video.

He sat up. There had to be other clues there. He took the tape he was yet to return to Celia and slipped it into the player.

The grainy video appeared. Slim sat back on the bed, watching the series of home video snippets play. Amos featured most; in the farmyard, in his workshop. Sometimes walking among the trees below the farm. Mary was almost wholly absent save for a couple of interruptions, while Charlotte was a silent, mostly immobile presence in Amos Birch's arms, or sitting close while he worked.

Slim frowned. There was something he wasn't seeing. He glared at the screen, wishing he could sort his thoughts into focus.

And then there it was. The elephant in the room; the balloon being waved in front of his eyes that he had been leaning around all this time, refusing to accept it. He let out a deflated cry, reaching for his coat and phone at the same time. He needed to talk to Kay.

He needed to talk to Kay now.

46

'WHAT THE HELL TIME DO YOU CALL THIS?' KAY SAID, sounding tired and irate at the same time. 'Can't it wait until the morning, Slim?'

Slim looked at his watch, but his watch was gone, perhaps left in his room. It was dark, but a clear sky and near full moon illuminated the distant mound of Bodmin Moor, a spectral sea rising up along the horizon, the lumpy tors lost and abandoned boats lifted on its wake.

He didn't remember how it had come to be night. It didn't matter.

'Kay. It's about that video I sent you. I need to clarify a few things.'

'Now? I was in the middle of something.'

'Look, I'm sorry. It won't take a minute. I just need to know why you found it creepy. It's a video of a family, isn't it? A girl, an old man, a mother in a wheelchair, a child. Right?'

'Jesus, how much have you drunk? It's going to kill you one day, Slim. Don't forget that.'

'Tell me, Kay! Are you seeing what I'm seeing?'

'You're as blinkered as an old horse. Yeah, I saw a family. A pretty messed up one. A girl's voice behind a camera, a middle-aged guy acting kind of awkward in front of it, and a sour-faced crone in a chair, but that other … what's this about, Slim?'

'Her name's Charlotte. She's the three-year-old daughter of Celia Birch and she's been missing since the night the old man disappeared.'

Kay let out a long whistle. 'Oh, Slim. I don't know what that is, but it's not a child.'

47

HE DIDN'T REMEMBER GETTING BACK TO THE guesthouse, only that it was morning and he was slumped against the wall on Mrs. Greyson's back veranda, clutching an empty bottle of whisky he had taken from her cabinet. The sun was rising over the trees at the end of her garden, and birds were singing from the rooftop.

He sat up, his vision blurring as his stomach lurched. He reached out, and found Mrs. Greyson's antique cast iron clock on the veranda beside him, the time saying a little after six thirty.

It was an effort to get up. It was an effort to get back through the kitchen, to replace the clock on the mantle in the exact same place and to hide the bottle behind a couple of others. It was even an effort to close the front door he had left wide open, at the same moment as a voice came from the top of the stairs.

'Mr. Hardy?'

Slim muttered something in response but neither his brain nor his ears could be sure what it was.

'An early morning walk?'

Another mumble.

Mrs. Greyson gave a slow nod. 'Well, I'll call you down in a couple of hours when the breakfast things are ready.'

'Thanks.'

It was a relief to shut himself back up in his room again. He sat on the edge of the bed, head in his hands. Cracks were appearing, threatening his sanity. Even though the revelation

(there was no child there was no child)

was another piece of the puzzle, Slim felt prematurely haunted by whatever else he might have missed.

After a breakfast where every bite left him with the urge to vomit despite Mrs. Greyson's charitable and surreptitious leaving of a couple of paracetamol under his plate, he returned to his room and switched the video back on.

Unblinkered now, it was obvious. Amos Birch, stooping as he carried her, as though Charlotte far exceeded the weight of a small child, talking to an object which never spoke back. There was movement though; the jerk of her head as though feigning interest, the lifting of her arms, the idle kicking of her feet. The clothes Charlotte wore suggested nothing and hid greater clues, but her skin was too smooth, too pale, and attracted a slight shine from the workshop lights.

A mechanical doll. Perhaps her movements worked

on voice command, or through the operating of tiny levers. The video clips never showed her close up, and from a distance her proportions were perfectly aligned to those of a three-year-old girl.

Celia had lied. There was no way she could have genuinely believed that a doll—no matter how lifelike—was her daughter.

Slim glanced up at the suitcase standing behind the door. It would be easy to pack his things and be up country in a few hours. He would never have to think about the Birch family again.

There was no bus to Tavistock on a Sunday, but if ever there was a day when Celia would be at home, it was now. He packed some things into a rucksack and headed out.

His hangover didn't appreciate Bodmin Moor, but his battered liver likely did. It was a stupid plan, one that could only be devised by a drunkard viewing the world through an alcoholic haze, but he figured the A30 was his best bet for thumbing a lift, and the quickest way to reach it was straight across Bodmin Moor.

It was after lunch before he made it, tired and wet as he stumbled through the door of Jamaica Inn and immediately ordered a pint and whatever was the food special for the day.

From a lay-by on the other side of the road he attempted to hitchhike. After a fruitless hour of frantic thumb waving, certain no one would be desperate enough for conversation to pick up what must have looked like a homeless alcoholic, he caught a lift with a farmer from Stoke Climsland. Slim feigned interest as the farmer chatted amicably about the weather and his two working children, before dropping Slim off at the top of a farm lane a couple of miles outside Tavistock.

It was dark by the time he reached Celia's street, and he felt as though he'd traversed the world a couple of times already as he trudged up to her door.

He was in no mood for subtlety. He made sure no one was nearby, then pulled the bolt cutters from his bag and jammed a protruding hook between the door and the jamb, breaking the lock with a loud crack.

He had read somewhere that the average response time for the U.K.'s police was eleven minutes, so he had just enough time to check if Celia was inside.

A quick flick of the switch inside the door told him the electric still worked. It revealed a neat if plain kitchen. No adornments, no pictures or photos on the fridge or walls, nothing to suggest anyone lived here.

He switched off the light again, preferring to use a torch he had brought. He opened a cupboard, finding it empty besides a few packets of pasta and some unopened biscuits. The fridge was similarly bare, containing a single carton of milk. The sell-by date was the same day Slim had last seen her.

A door opened on to a plain living room. There was no TV. Two armchairs angled towards each other faced an empty coffee table. One looked used, its seat depressed, the arms a little worn. The other looked new. Like the kitchen there were no pictures on the walls, nothing personal of any kind. Slim walked through it, careful not to touch anything, and opened an inner door.

The room was dark, the curtains drawn. The shape of a bed revealed itself as a rectangular black lump, one not straight to the wall but partly pulled away as though someone had needed to get behind it.

And here, finally, were signs of disorder, of clothes strewn across the floor, bottles of shampoo and hairspray alongside empty beer cans and even a cardboard Pringles tube. Scattered across everything were pieces of paper, their corners torn where pins had remained embedded into walls when they were ripped free.

He switched on the light. Several dozen grainy images of a doll's face stared back at him, taken from a paused TV screen with a camera and then printed and enlarged on a colour copier. Slim felt his stomach lurch. His knees trembled and he squatted before the shock made him fall.

'Oh, Celia,' he whispered.

NOW THE PARAMETERS OF HIS SEARCH COULD BE narrowed, tracking down Celia was far easier.

It took him just three calls to find her. Not a nurse as she claimed, but a patient at Melton Road Private Psychiatric Hospital, where she had been a resident of one kind or another since 1997, the year after her father's disappearance.

A doctor told Slim—posing as a family friend—that Celia had been an outpatient since early 2006, living in a care-assisted flat in Tavistock, allowed to sleep there three nights a week, and even to hold a part time job in a local factory.

Her illness: delusional schizophrenia. The doctor explained that since her mid-teens Celia had struggled with an understanding of what was real and what was not. Certain things, he said, triggered or perhaps suppressed by traumatic events, had left her believing aspects of her life were real, when in fact they were creations of her own imagination.

Charlotte. Her life as a nurse. Perhaps even her rape.

'I need to see her,' he said. 'It's important.'

There was a pause on the other end of the line. Slim's head spun as he waited for the doctor's words.

'I'm afraid that's not possible. A few days ago she was in an accident.'

Slim listened in shock as the doctor recounted that Celia, banned from driving, had overturned a stolen Ford Fiesta while fleeing from police. It turned out she was also responsible for a prior recent theft of a 1994 Rover Metro, a car which had been found abandoned on a farm lane not far outside Tavistock.

Slim squeezed his eyes shut, wishing he could turn back the clock.

'Where is she now?'

'Derriford Hospital. The intensive care unit.'

After calling off and steadying his nerves with a can of beer from a corner shop, Slim tried to call Don, to hold off the savaging of Nick's career, but got no answer. Instead, he called the hospital and asked to speak to Celia.

A little stricter about giving out personal information than the psychiatric hospital had been, Slim spent a few minutes convincing the staff member he spoke to that he was a distant relative. Finally he was put through to a doctor, who told him Celia had suffered head injuries in the crash. She was unconscious, unlikely to recover.

He wandered around Tavistock in a daze. The bench which had been his bed the previous night became his crutch where he sat and drank, descending through levels of pitifulness until a man with a shaggy beard, shabbier clothes, and gummy eyes asked him why he was crying and offered to share a bottle of White Lightning.

Everything had fallen apart. Slim tried to recall if he had helped a single person with his investigation, and came up with a negative. He had been warned away so many times, but he had kept digging, kept cracking his head against the wall which had now collapsed. As a result, Celia, who might have known a modicum of peace before his interference, lay dying.

Amos Birch, he saw now, had done what he could to help his daughter. Traumatised by some event, he had created a mechanical doll to fill a void in his daughter's life.

'He built it for her,' he mumbled to the drunk, who nodded sagely. 'He built that thing to help her.'

'Bit much,' the drunk said. 'Could've just gone down Tesco's, bought one of them Disney dolls. Girl must have been messed up a bit worse, if you ask me.'

'Yeah, she was.'

'Wonder why, eh.'

'What?'

'Ain't many mothers send a lass mental. Never knew mine, but you know. Must have been some trauma.'

Sure that the drunk was humouring what he likely regarded as a drunken lament, Slim felt another click on the cog slowly rolling him into the dark.

He took a last swig of White Lightning while the drunk beside him babbled on about social services, then

Slim sat up. He passed the bottle back, thinking about Charlotte.

There was more. There had to be.

Excusing himself, he headed back into town, hoping he hadn't missed the last bus to Plymouth.

49

Slim clutched the photocopy in his hands. A single beaded tear slowly spread itself out, burrowing into the paper. It had landed on Celia's name, and the C was slowly expanding, the ink blooming like an algae spot in a pond.

Merrifield, Charlotte Ann
Mother: Merrifield, Celia Father: unknown
Born June 19th, 1992.
Died June 19th, 1992.
Cause of death: stillbirth.

Slim read the information over and over. Each time his eyes traced over the brief lines he felt another piece of his sanity stripping away.

And if it was so hard for him, how had it been for Celia?

There had been a baby after all. A tiny little girl who

had died in the womb, never to open her innocent little eyes.

Charlotte Merrifield.

Charlotte Birch.

Slim called Derrifield Hospital, asking about visiting hours to see Celia, but was told she was still in intensive care, still unresponsive. He was welcome to come to the hospital, but her room was off limits.

He felt like getting drunk then trying to force his way into her room to say he was sorry, but he was tiring of the mess he was making of himself. There had to be something positive he could do that might actually help.

Amos Birch had taken Charlotte with him when he had gone to hide his unfinished clock from the wrath of his wife. If the clock was buried out on Bodmin Moor, it made sense that Charlotte was too.

Bodmin Moor was vast. Slim would never find it. Unless….

No more buses. He was done with cramped seats, twisting country lanes and long pauses pressed against the hedge while a tractor squeezed past. He had a credit card, so it was time to see if it still worked.

He visited a hardware store to purchase a durable spade then he went back outside and hailed down a taxi.

50

He had to wait until late afternoon, until the shadows stretching over the moor were in a similar position to those he remembered on the day he had found the clock before he could get his bearings. Even though he found the rocky area west of the path where he had tripped, he was still wandering among the stones for a good half an hour, wondering if he would ever find the right spot again, before stumbling across a disturbed patch of ground where a finger of torn plastic bag still fluttered out of the earth.

Here.

He pushed the spade slowly into the ground until it met resistance. Then, using the spade's head and his hands, he scraped away the peat to reveal the object that had been buried below the clock.

The wooden casket had been wrapped in cellophane which had torn, allowing the water to soak and stain the wood. It still felt sturdy, however, and when Slim pulled the heavy box out of the earth, something inside gave a dry rattle.

The lid had been fitted water-tight. Slim used the edge of the spade to pry it open, his fingers shaking as he lifted it up.

The last rays of the evening sun caught Charlotte's face as Slim tilted the box to see inside. He gasped, almost dropping it as the girl's eyes flicked open

(it's a doll a doll a doll)

and the head tilted in his direction, neat layers of metal beside its mouth clicking back to form a pretty smile.

He let out a sharp breath. An automaton, a vintage mechanical toy, operated by hundreds of cogs and levers hidden inside its body cavity. The doll had shifted in the box, setting off a process which altered its expression. As the eyes blinked again and the smile fell back into an expressionless place, Slim gulped, feeling as though he had woken his own monster.

He stared at it for a few seconds, but nothing else happened. Movement had activated it. Careful not to move the box, Slim reached in to touch Charlotte's face.

Whether Amos Birch had built the doll from scratch or simply acquired an old one to restore, Slim might never know. The craftsmanship was exquisite, every surface perfectly aligned. Up close its face was a series of shifting plates which could move to display emotion, but it only took a slight relaxing of his vision to blur Charlotte's face into that of a real girl.

He reached in and lifted the doll out of the box. Most of Charlotte's body was wooden, but as she shifted in Slim's arms the click and ping of thousands of clockwork mechanisms came from inside.

'You made it for her, didn't you?' Slim whispered. 'You built it to ease your daughter's pain … and maybe even your own.'

51

DERRIFORD HOSPITAL WAS, AS ALL HOSPITALS WERE, endless corridors with too many doors and unpronounceable signs leading to waiting rooms packed with glum people watching daytime TV or reading magazines months out of date. Slim made his way through the labyrinth to the intensive care unit where he sought out a duty doctor.

There were times when it was best to wear a disguise and others when total honesty was most important. Slim stripped himself down layer by layer, telling the doctor how he'd come to Cornwall to recover from his own problems but had got involved with the mystery of Amos Birch's disappearance, which eventually led him to Celia. Had he known she was stealing cars to meet him he would have left her alone, and he blamed himself for her accident.

With the doctor's ear turning toward sympathy, Slim produced Charlotte's box and announced that he had found an old treasure belonging to Celia and wondered if he could spend a few minutes by her side.

His request was granted, provided a nurse was allowed to wait by the door. Slim agreed. The doctor led him along the corridor into a bright but plain room with a view over farmland to the south. Celia, only her eyes and mouth visible through bandages, was hooked up to a series of machines which bleeped with a comforting regularity.

'Is she expected to wake?' he asked the nurse.

The woman gave a sad shake of her head. 'We're just making her comfortable,' she said. 'She wasn't wearing a seatbelt.'

Slim nodded. He took a chair beside the bed and lifted the box onto his knees.

'Hello, Celia,' he said, reaching out to touch her hand. Her skin felt rubbery under his fingers, and when his arm brushed against the tube inserted into a vein in her arm he had to close his eyes a moment to control his emotions.

'It's Slim,' he said, when he felt sure he could speak without breaking down. 'I just wanted to say that I'm sorry for everything that happened. I made a mistake. I should have left your family alone. I really thought I could find out what happened to your father, but I didn't realise the damage I could cause by digging up the past. I truly regret it.'

He took a deep breath, concentrating on keeping his voice level. He glanced at the nurse, who gave him a sympathetic smile.

'I just wanted to say that meeting you affected me

deeply. I'm a lonely, failing man, and a huge part of me regrets with all my heart turning down your offer, and not because it may have led to you lying here, but because I recognised in you what I've often seen in myself. However, you've been broken in a different way, and I don't think my heart could have fixed you.'

He paused, looking out of the window at a distant aeroplane vapour trail, remembering how Amos Birch's letter had said how much he despised flying.

'I haven't found your father.'

Was there a slight flutter of her eyelids? Slim pulled his chair a little closer and cleared his throat.

'Sometimes people aren't meant to be found. But I did find out who hurt you that night. He was a man who you should have been able to trust, and I will do everything in my power to ensure that he is brought to justice. And….' He paused again. 'I found Charlotte. I brought her back to you. She's right here with me now.'

This time there was a definite flutter of her eyelids. Slim's heart raced as he opened the box and lifted out the doll. Charlotte moved with a series of clicks as Slim sat her up on his lap.

'Charlotte … she's right here, Celia. Just as you remember. Your daughter. Your father loved you so much. He always loved you, Celia. I found that out for sure. He never planned to leave you, but circumstances were out of his control. Before he left, though, he made sure Charlotte was safe, and she has been, all these years. She's just as you remember her. She hasn't changed at all. I'm going to let you hold her, Celia. Is that okay?'

He stood up. The nurse made to get up too, but Slim gave her a smile and waved for her to sit.

Lifting Charlotte carefully, he lowered her on to the bed, moving Celia's arm so that Charlotte could nestle into the crutch of Celia's armpit. He lifted her fingers and laid them across Charlotte's stomach.

'Goodbye, Celia.'

He paused a moment before he turned away, and in that second he saw a slight creasing of Celia's lips into the faintest of smiles. Across Charlotte's stomach, her fingers gave a slight flex.

As Slim turned, he saw the nurse dabbing her eyes with a tissue.

'Thank you,' she whispered.

He went for a walk around pleasant grounds set around the hospital's car park. His mind was reeling and he couldn't keep the tears from his eyes. All he could see was Celia, lying in the hospital bed.

Unsure what else to do, eventually he gravitated back to the hospital, where he found a quiet waiting room and bought a coffee from a vending machine. He sat down on a plastic chair and switched on his phone.

Don had left a voicemail.

'Sorry, Slim, I owe you an apology. I cracked that phone you sent me, and it contained some decent dirt. Some pretty inappropriate emails to minors, stuff like that. I made some notes and mailed it back to you. Unfortunately I screwed up your address and accidentally sent it to a tabloid newspaper. Man, I'm such a fool. Laters.'

Slim smiled. So, Nick would see justice after all. He

was just thinking to call Don back to thank him when he looked up to see the nurse from Celia's room standing over him.

'Mr. Hardy, there you are.'

As he looked at her expectantly, she gave a regretful shake of her head. 'I'm afraid Celia passed shortly after you left,' she said. 'I'm so sorry. I just wanted to let you know that I think you gave her peace before she died. Many patients don't get that. Thank you, Mr. Hardy.'

He wanted to reply, but no words would come. Instead, he pulled the nurse into an embrace, sobbing into her shoulder.

52

PENLEVEN WAS AS QUIET AS USUAL ON WHAT SLIM decided would be his last day. Celia Birch was two days cremated, her ashes interred into a small casket in a quiet corner of Penleven's churchyard. At Slim's insistence both Charlotte's doll and Amos's final clock had been cremated with her, letting her go to her eternal rest with memories of the two most important people in her life.

Slim, after struggling with his guilt following Celia's death, was slowly finding a renewed optimism.

Three days now since he had chosen to stay dry for Celia's funeral—a low key affair where his presence had raised a few eyebrows from people whom he hadn't expected to see either—and he felt as though he might have survived his jaunt in the country more or less intact.

With his mind cleared out, it had been easier to

think about the original mystery—that of Amos Birch's disappearance.

No one ever vanished. They always went somewhere.

He stood up as he spotted June further up the street, leading a scraggly poodle which seemed intent on sticking its nose into every patch of grass they passed.

'I didn't know you had a dog,' he said.

June shrugged. 'Got her yesterday from the rescue centre in Wadebridge. Thought I'd do something good for the world.'

Slim smiled. 'What's her name?'

'Reg.'

At Slim's look of alarm, June laughed. 'Not really. Rose.'

'Pretty.'

'You don't look busy, Slim. I don't suppose you'd still be interested in that tea?'

Slim smiled. 'I'm afraid I'm leaving today.'

June looked momentarily crestfallen, but recovered with a smile. 'I'll miss you, Slim. The Crown won't be the same without you riling up the regulars and nearly starting fights.'

'Ah, you'll forget all about me,' he said. 'You have Rose to look after you now.'

'And she's a damn sight more reliable, I'm sure.' June shrugged. She gave him that awkward look that suggested she wanted to both stay with him and hurry away.

'So, you didn't find him, then?'

'Amos?' Slim shook his head. 'No.'

June stood awkwardly a moment then started forward, kissing Slim on the cheek. She gave his hand a squeeze before backing away, tugged by Rose nosing into the hedgerow.

'Some people aren't meant to be found,' she said. 'See you, Slim.'

He watched her go. She didn't look back.

'Not yet,' he muttered then turned away, heading back up through the village.

53

He had left his cases standing in the hallway at the guesthouse before going down to the village. When he entered, the sound of the TV came muffled through the closed living room door. The postman had recently been so he picked Mrs. Greyson's letters off the mat and knocked on the door.

Mrs. Greyson was sitting in her chair, watching the BBC local news. Slim caught a glimpse of a scrolling headline—*Local teacher forced to resign amidst fresh allegations of sexual misconduct as further witnesses come forward*—before Mrs. Greyson stood up. She waved a TV remote behind her and the TV cut off, but not before a brief shot of the exterior of Liskeard Secondary.

'So, you're leaving today, Mr. Hardy? I'm going to miss you, believe it or not. You've become the good-for-nothing son I can't help but spoil.'

Slim smiled, then nodded. 'I think I've done all I can here. I came here to recover, but only time will tell if I'm leaving in a worse state than I arrived.' He shrugged. 'You have to do what you have to do, don't you? To survive, to get by. I'm sure you know that as well as anyone, don't you, Mrs. Greyson?'

She nodded. 'It was never easy living with Roy. I survived as best I could.'

'But once you dreamed of better, didn't you?'

She shrugged, turning back to the TV. 'Well, probably.'

'I know you did. It didn't work out though, did it, Mrs. Greyson? Or can I call you Mary?'

He held out the letters he had picked up by the door, brushing her shoulder as she jerked back around. She lifted her glasses to look at them, each one addressed to Mary Greyson of Lakeview Guesthouse, Penleven, Cornwall.

'I don't—'

Slim let her take them from his hand then walked over to the mantelpiece and lifted the heavy cast iron clock, turning it over in his hands.

'It's always run slow, you told me. I imagine something like this would. It must be what, a hundred years old?'

'It belonged to my grandfather, the accursed thing.'

'Amos Birch used to come here and fix it, didn't he? I heard he used to fix clocks around the village from time to time.'

'It was the only way he could get that woman to let him out.'

Slim turned to face Mrs. Greyson. She was sitting up in the chair, her letters forgotten in her hand.

'A clock like this, I imagine it needed regular maintenance. Over time the two of you became close, didn't you?'

Mrs. Greyson was staring at him. 'I don't know what you're insinuating, Mr. Hardy. We were friends, but that's all. He needed time away from that … that tyrant, and my Roy was never one for caring what I did when he was away. Amos and I bonded in our collective unhappiness.'

Slim ran a finger over the dent in the lower surface of the clock, that made it jostle rather than sit straight.

'He made you happy, didn't he? Until the night he came to tell you he was going away for a while, and asked you to keep a couple of items safe.'

A tear ran down Mrs. Greyson's cheek.

'How did you…?'

'He told you he was going away, and you got angry. You didn't want him to leave.'

Slim lifted the clock cracked it against his palm, making Mrs. Greyson jump. She was openly crying now. Letters scattered across the floor as she gripped her cheeks. 'How could you know?'

Slim replaced the clock on the mantel. He sighed. 'I didn't, not for sure. It was a guess until you told me. Sit down, Mrs. Greyson. I'll make you some tea.'

She didn't move. Her armchair became her prison as she stared helplessly at the clock, rocking slightly as it ticked away, heavy, lethargic movements like slaps across a person's face. Slim watched her for a moment then went off into the kitchen, feeling equal parts of relief and regret.

54

SLIM HANDED A CUP TO MRS. GREYSON. IT TREMBLED against the saucer as she took it, looking up at him with fearful eyes.

'Tell me what happened,' Slim said, taking an armchair opposite. 'Please. I need to know as much as I think you need to tell it.'

Mrs. Greyson set the cup down. She dabbed her eyes with a handkerchief. 'Have you ever truly loved anyone, Mr. Hardy?'

Slim gave a slow nod. 'Yes, I have. It didn't work out so well. When I think back on it now, I'm not sure whether I'd prefer it to never have happened or not.'

'Then maybe you can understand. Amos … we got friendly over that stupid old clock. He used to come here and wind it. He was a magician. It was as though it spoke to him. Silly thing would never work properly for me.'

Slim nodded. 'I hear he was one of the best.'

'Oh, he could do wonders with any machine. Not like my … well, we got friendly, but I swear that's all it was. I thought that was all it was, but he was lonely, and I….' She smiled, sobbing at the same time. 'I was a lot younger then, too. Some might have said pretty.'

'And your relationship was mutual?'

'He used to come over all the time when Roy was away. He'd come across the field and over the back hedge so no one would see him, and we … I hoped he might leave his wife, but he said he never would. Not so much for her, but for Celia, the poor girl.'

'What did you know of her?'

'Only that she wasn't of sound mind. That she had problems. We didn't talk about it. He came to forget his problems, and when he was here I wanted to forget mine.'

Again she sniffed into her handkerchief. Slim waited patiently, sipping tea that tasted impotent without an alcoholic kick.

'And then he came over one night, out of the blue, to say he was going away. We argued. I told him not to leave. He claimed he would come back, but I saw a lie in his eyes. He started to leave, and I picked up that clock, and I said … I said….'

Her hands were shaking. Slim got out of his chair and knelt in front of her, holding her hands gently in his.

'Please tell me,' he said.

'I said, don't you just walk away from me … and I threw it. I meant to hit the door. It should have hit the door. But he turned back. Right at the last moment, he turned….'

240

Slim gently patted her hands while she cried. For several minutes she couldn't find the will to speak, but gradually the sobbing subsided.

'I killed him,' she said. 'I killed the only man I ever truly loved, and I've had to live with it for every waking moment since.'

Slim nodded. 'You told me you were good at hiding things,' he said. 'When the police came….'

'I'd had time to get myself together. It was a couple of days after. I thought they might have suspected, that they'd hear a lie in my voice, but they never came back.'

'Where was he?'

'I hid the body in the vegetable cellar under the house. There was a blood stain on the floorboard in the hall, but they never even noticed.'

'Where is he now?'

'I buried him under the tree at the end of the garden. The one he gave … the one he … gave me….'

Mrs. Greyson began to cry again. 'The lime tree,' Slim said. 'I thought I recognised it. There are others at Worth Farm. They're about the same size. You buried the clock and the doll too, didn't you?'

Mrs Greyson nodded. 'After the search was over, I took them up to the moor. I knew how much Amos loved Bodmin Moor. I found a spot from where you can see both coasts on a clear day.'

'And every so often you go up to wind the clock?'

Mrs. Greyson sniffed. 'Just something I do to keep his memory alive. One of many things. But when you found it, it started to mess with my head. How did you know, Mr. Hardy?'

Slim shrugged. 'I'd never make a real detective,' he said. 'I'd burn vital evidence or sleep with a witness. I'm not even good at private investigation work. I miss obvious stuff, I ask intrusive questions, I go on whims, and I trust my intuition more than is safe. Sometimes, however, something just clicks, as though I were wired wrong.'

He let go of her hands and went back to his chair, lifting his cup to swallow the last of his tea.

'Things began to stand out. He started to write you a note, but decided to tell you in person, at the same time hoping to entrust you with his important items. After what I'd heard of Mary Birch it didn't make sense that he'd be writing to her. I'd seen your name on letters in the hall, but it didn't all snap together. Then there was the clock, the tree, that you went out at night, that you drank yourself to sleep after opening my mail … I should have realised earlier.'

Both were silent for a while. Slim listened to a car speed past, a bird singing from the gutter. Finally, Mrs. Greyson said, 'What happens now? Will we go to the station, or will the police come here? I don't think I could handle prison, Mr. Hardy, but it's what I deserve.'

Slim gave her a sad smile. 'I once tried to kill a man,' he said. 'I thought he was sleeping with my wife. I went after him with a razor blade, but I'd been drinking. I cut him a couple of times, but he was Armed Forces. He knocked me down, kept me that way until the police showed up. He got off with a couple of minor cuts. For my part, I was discharged from the Armed Forces and got away with a suspended sentence for ABH. Had I showed up sober I might have got twenty years for murder.'

'Why are you telling me this?'

'Because I tried to kill a man, and I'm here sitting opposite you, free. Which of us most deserves to do time? You've been suffering over this for twenty-two years. You lost the man you loved. I think that's sentence enough.'

'So you—'

Slim stood up as a car pulled up outside. 'That's my taxi. Could you help me with my cases?'

Mrs. Greyson opened her mouth to speak then closed it again. Silently she nodded, following him out into the hall.

'I enjoyed my stay,' Slim said, turning back, after his bags were loaded. 'I mean that. I really did. You make the best hangover coffee I think I've ever had. It was certainly a stay I'll never forget.'

'Thank you,' Mr. Hardy, Mrs. Greyson said. 'Thank you for understanding.'

Slim nodded. He looked up at the sky, one of the clearest he'd seen since coming here, and smiled. Then he climbed into the taxi. As it pulled away, he glanced back and saw Mrs. Greyson lift a brief hand in farewell. She watched for a moment, then lowered her head, turned, and disappeared up the path.

Penleven was soon behind him as the taxi wound its way out of the valleys surrounding Bodmin Moor. Slim caught a brief glimpse of Rough Tor as the taxi passed a gateway, then it too was gone, and Slim realised he really wouldn't mind if he never saw the wilds of Bodmin Moor again.

It was over. He, at least, and perhaps Mrs. Greyson, had found closure. Just one thing still bothered him.

The note.

He took the sheaf of papers out from his bag and looked over the pictures of the clock, then the samples of handwriting. It was so obvious now. The thin panel along the lower part of the clock face that looked like a moon had been designed for a carved inscription, and the single line of text had been meant as an epitaph.

But what of the markings? They didn't match the first line, but what about the second, the barely legible one Kay had been unable to decipher? Amos had left the carving unfinished, but as Slim peered at the photocopy, he found himself frowning.

'You enjoy your stay down in these parts?' the taxi driver said abruptly, breaking Slim out of his thoughts.

'It was … peaceful,' he said.

'Quite,' the driver responded. 'You picked a nice part of the county. Not many tourists round here and you can't get more Cornish than old Bodmin Moor.'

Slim nodded. On the dashboard, a smartphone fitted into a stand suddenly flicked into life with a GPS system as it picked up a signal. Slim stared at it, wondering.

'I don't suppose I could borrow your phone for a moment?' he asked. 'I'd like to look something up.'

The driver plucked the phone out of the cradle and passed it back. 'Sure. I think I know where I am by now.'

With a few clicks, Slim brought up an online translator. With the paper showing the note balanced on one knee, he input a couple of words until what he was hoping for appeared on the screen.

'Well, I never.'

'All right back there?'

'Are you familiar with the Cornish language at all?' Slim asked the driver.

'I'm afraid not. Come from Tiverton myself, over the border. Place names and all that, and of course Kernow from the welcome sign. That's about it, though.'

'Thanks.'

Slim looked down at the phone, then at the paper, the two words from the second line that were visible. "Amper" meant "time" in Cornish, while what had looked to Kay like "puppy" could actually be "pupprys," the Cornish word for "forever".

Then, of course, there was the initial at the end of the lower line. The A, Slim now saw, wasn't an A nor even an M as Kay had suggested, but looked that way because of water expansion and a little tear which had twisted the paper around.

It had once been a K.

It took only a couple of minutes to figure out what the K could have stood for.

Keugh sira-wynn.

Cornish for "grandfather".

'It wasn't just Celia who was struggling with her grief, was it?' Slim muttered, lining up one of Amos's letters to Herr Schwimmer to compare the handwriting against the note. He sighed. The resemblance was uncanny. 'You were grieving too. You lost your only grandchild. You planned to hide your memorial behind a language no one around you would understand.'

Charlotte. Your time is forever. I will wait for you always. Grandfather.

Slim put the papers away as the car pulled up to the junction with the A39. A lorry trailer rumbled past, followed by a frustrated line of cars.

'Thanks for the loan,' Slim said, handing the phone back to the driver, who slipped it back into its cradle.'

'Which bus station you want, mate?' the driver said. 'You want Camelford or should I head to Bude?'

Slim smiled. 'Whichever one is closest,' he said.

Thank you for reading!
If you enjoyed reading this ebook,
please consider buying me a coffee!
All supporters will get a mention
in the back of the next Slim Hardy Mystery!

The Games Keeper - The Slim Hardy Mysteries #3

THANK YOU FOR READING!

The adventures of Slim Hardy continue in

The Games Keeper

Available Now

ABOUT THE AUTHOR

Jack Benton is a pen name of Chris Ward, the author of the dystopian *Tube Riders* series, the horror/science fiction *Tales of Crow* series, and the *Endinfinium* YA fantasy series, as well as numerous other well-received stand alone novels.

The Clockmaker's Secret is the second mystery to feature Slim Hardy. There will be more…

Chris would love to hear from you:
www.amillionmilesfromanywhere.net/tokyolost
chrisward@amillionmilesfromanywhere.net

ACKNOWLEDGMENTS

Big thanks as always to those of you who provided help and encouragement. My proofreader Jenny, and the guys at The Cover Collection get a special heads up, as does as always, my muse, Jenny Twist.

In addition, extra thanks goes to my Patreon supporters, in particular to Amaranth Dawe, Charles Urban, Janet Hodgson, Juozas Kasiulis, Leigh McEwan, and Teri L. Ruscak.

You guys are awesome.